CW01546215

MURDER AT THE HALLOWEEN PARTY

Totally Addictive Cozy Mystery

Massachusetts Cozy Mystery
Book 10

ANDREA KRESS

Chapter 1

Amanda waited in the vestibule of Boston's Museum of Fine Art looking out on the statue of the warrior on horseback with his arms outstretched to the sky. While she always admired the artistry, at that moment it was a metaphor for her feelings toward her sister who had dramatically summoned her without explanation yet was once again late. She looked back and forth on Huntington Avenue and, after another ten minutes, saw a taxi pull up and Louisa leisurely step out and come up the long walk.

"Thanks for meeting me," Louisa said. "I needed a bit of art today and somebody to share it with."

"That's it? And Rob wasn't available?" Amanda asked, referring to her brother-in-law.

"He's always got something going on at the club. I had to twist his arm to get him to carve out dinner with me every day but the weekends."

"Such is married life," Amanda said, herself recently wed.

"I guess I never noticed how hard he worked, especially when I was there with him."

"What is the occasion today for your need for art?"

"Monsieur Josef thought I was spending too much time at the salon, either sketching or showing designs to the customers, and should be out and about for inspiration. He suggested that I take in the Sargent portraits, in particular. They're elegant and floor length and he has the idea that women will want to go back to the styles of the past century."

"Really? Does he think that we want to get into corsets, trussed up like a chicken ready for the oven?"

"I don't think he meant that exactly. More like the vertical lines and simplicity of the dresses. He loathes all the buttons and bows that people are favoring these days. And I quite agree. Entirely too fussy for the modern woman."

"That's a nice employer you've got! I can tell you Daddy has never made such a suggestion to me to take the day off and browse in a museum," Amanda said, referring to her own work as a private investigator at her father's law firm.

Louisa tucked her arm under her sister's and they walked toward the rotunda. Louisa pulled away and twirled around looking at the John Singer Sargent frescoes on the walls and ceiling.

"I just love his work and his portraits. It would have been wonderful to have had him paint me."

"Two problems," Amanda said. "He died when you were quite young. And even if he wished to paint a little girl—and he did many times quite masterfully—the family couldn't have afforded it."

"Oh, to be rich," Louisa sighed.

"Hello," said a voice from one of the entrances.

"Bitsy!" Louisa exclaimed, rushing toward her friend and giving her an embrace. "What are you doing here?"

Her fellow former debutante, short in stature as her nickname implied, pulled a portfolio from under her arm. "Sketching. Hello, Amanda."

"How exciting! Let's see," Louisa said.

"Spencer is so busy with his real estate business that I'm just kicking around the house all day by myself. So, I decided to take an art class. They have us visiting museums and sketching masterpieces. I'm just a beginner," she said, turning open the cover to reveal a landscape with a partly crumbling castle in the background.

"You have talent," Louisa said.

"It's lovely," Amanda agreed.

"Thank you," Bitsy said. "Come into the next gallery to sit and we can talk."

"Tell us about Spencer's business," Louisa said.

"He has what they call 'listings' where owners sign up with an agent—he's a broker—to try to sell their property. He's got some extraordinary homes listed, but they are large and expensive and in this Depression climate, even if people could afford it, they're hesitant."

"True," Amanda said. "I've overheard conversations at my father's firm with clients who didn't really suffer in the Crash, but who are hesitant to do anything out of the ordinary for fear of the repercussions."

"What sort of homes does he have listed?" Louisa asked.

"The Van Eaton property, for one."

"I know that one," Amanda said. "It's almost around the corner from us. I've seen the sign out front. Sad history."

"That may be why no one wants to buy it, although it comes with all the furniture."

"That might sound like an incentive if it's the right kind of furniture," Louisa said. "You'd have a hard time unloading that heavy stuff that our grandparents had."

Amanda paused as her mind was working quickly, thinking about possibilities.

"And then the old Williams place. You know, that pile up the hill," Bitsy said.

"I always thought that was some sort of castle. Very distinct," Louisa said.

"That's one way of putting it. Spencer has had a heck of a time even getting someone in to see it." Bitsy glanced at her watch. "I'd better be going. Let's be sure to stay in touch. It was so nice seeing both of you," she said, getting up and dashing toward the exit.

Amanda looked at her sister, who had a faraway look in her eyes. "What's going on in that brain of yours?"

"Some wonderful ideas. Spencer needs to bring in young, vibrant, wealthy people to see the house, not middle-aged couples. And I have just the idea of how to do it."

As they walked through the galleries, Louisa expounded on her plan.

"We'll throw a Halloween costume party. Thirty under thirty--thirty people under the age of thirty. Up-and-coming movers and shakers with money to burn."

"After the Crash and with the recovery being so slow, do such people even exist anymore?"

"Of course. We might not hobnob with them, but they exist all right. The party will take place in the Williams house. To show it off to its best advantage. Music, champagne, games. But the best part is that costumes will be required. You know, for each couple, a King and a Queen. Sun and Moon. Caesar and Cleopatra."

"Peter Pan and Wendy. Holmes and Watson."

"Exactly. Naturally they will be referred to Monsieur Josef's salon for the costume creation. No homemade ghost costumes made with a sheet and two openings for the eyes. And, of course, you'll be invited. Doesn't that sound like a wonderful idea?"

"Yes, as long as Brendan and I are not the Cop and Robber couple."

"Of course not. We wouldn't want to typecast the charming and handsome Lieutenant Halloran as the Cop. Nor you as the Robber."

"Thank you," Amanda said with relief. "But Brendan is over thirty. Does that disqualify him?"

"No, we'll cut him and Rob some grace on the age requirement. I'll draw up a list of couples' costumes later tonight and you'll get first choice. Well, second choice after Rob and me. Won't this be the event of the year? And Spencer will be sure to sell that pile in no time." She snapped her fingers.

It sounded like an exciting plan. Who could imagine it would end in a murder?

Chapter 2

Amanda dropped her sister off and continued to the half of the duplex shared with Brendan, her mind swirling with ideas, and they weren't about the costume party. She was once again drawn to the idea of buying a house, and the Van Eaton property provided a rare opportunity. The main house had four bedrooms, which the former owner had rented out to his gentlemen friends, young fellows just starting out on their careers. There was an attached living unit with a separate entrance that might have belonged to the original owner's household staff and was significantly larger than the duplex where she currently lived. What intrigued her about the idea was that rental income from the big house could offset part of the mortgage.

Amanda parked in front of the duplex owned by Brendan's parents and saw that he hadn't come home yet. That would give her some time to jot down numbers, but first she had to tackle dinner. Growing up in a household with a proficient cook made her attempts seem amateurish by comparison. That, combined with seeing Brendan's mother whip up large quantities for her large family in the blink of an eye, intimidated her further. But armed with the cookbook that her parents' staff had given her as a wedding present, she was beginning to get comfortable with the idea of putting together a meal.

That night it was to be veal cutlets purchased the day before, canned peas and applesauce. Their family cook would have blanched at the thought of canned peas, but Amanda didn't have time during the usual workday to shop for fresh produce, much less to prepare it, which involved snapping off the ends and tearing open the pods to pull the peas out. And in a moment of vanity, she decided she was also not going to ruin a perfectly good manicure preparing vegetables. Canned peas it was. She took off her suit jacket, washed her hands and put on an apron. Leftover rice from the night before would be made into rice pudding if she had the time before Brendan came home. It was at such moments that she longed for the days when they went out for a restaurant dinner. But they were trying to live economically, a notion that had not been part of her experience growing up.

Amanda took the Fanny Farmer Cookbook from the shelf and looked at the veal cutlet recipe. She was supposed to pound them with a meat tenderizer. What the heck was that? She opened one of the utensil drawers and didn't see anything that fit the bill. She went back to the recipe and read that she could use the edge of a plate. She unwrapped the two cutlets, left them on the butcher paper and began methodically pounding the meat until it was thin. The next instruction was to have an egg and breadcrumbs in separate bowls. Having done so, she set them aside.

It wasn't yet time to prepare the main meal, so she began on the rice pudding, which was supposed to have the rice from scratch. That seemed wasteful when she had a good amount already cooked. Milk, an egg and raisins were the only other things needed. She looked in the cabinet. Of course, there were no raisins. Why would the bachelor Brendan have bought raisins? There was vanilla that she had purchased and cinnamon, and that would have to do. She cooked it on the small stovetop until it was creamy and set the pot aside to cool. She checked the time and saw that Brendan wouldn't be home for at least forty-five minutes, so she left the cutlets on the countertop and went to the telephone book in the hall, looked up Spencer Whiting's work number at Hammond & Whiting and dialed. Luckily, he was in, she introduced herself and peppered him with questions about the Van Eaton property.

"Are you ready to make an offer?" he asked, with a smile in his voice.

"Not yet. But thank you for the information."

With a sense of anticipation, she sat down at the dining room table, the only substitute for a desk that they had in their place. She began to work with the information he had provided and wrote out what she thought would be reasonable rent for tenants. Was that too little or too much? She had never been a renter and had no idea or what Brendan's parents charged them, which was probably below what others paid. Were they expected to pay for water, gas and electricity separately or was that included in the rent? Since the last owner had left the furniture behind at the Van Eaton house, renting it furnished would be an easier selling point for a prospective tenant, and they could charge more. She heard the key in the lock and quickly put the paper into the pocket of her apron.

"Hello," Brendan called out, taking off his hat and looking for her in the kitchen. "What smells so good?" he asked, giving her a kiss.

"Rice pudding for dessert."

"Sounds wonderful." He retraced his steps and put hat and coat on the coat rack just inside the front door.

"What else is for supper?" he asked when he returned and looked over to the small counter next to the stove. "Veal cutlets! My favorite. Are you making veal parmesan?"

Amanda blinked at him. "If you think I can put together a meal like Mrs. Russo at Catalano's, you are sadly mistaken. Let's hope that veal will still be your favorite when I get done with it," she answered.

"I see you have been consulting the oracle," he said picking up the cookbook.

"It will be years before I can put together a three-course meal for as many people as your mother does in the blink of an eye."

"She had a lot of practice helping her mother with a big family and boarders back then, to boot."

"Let me get started, then," Amanda said. With her back to him, she dipped the cutlets in the beaten egg and then into the breadcrumbs as she asked. "How was work?"

He took a glass from the cabinet and filled it with water from the tap. "Quiet today. That's not a good sign. It means all hell is likely to break loose soon."

"Why?"

"No reason. Just the way that things go. How was your tour of the museum?"

"Fine. It gave Louisa some interesting ideas." She put the cutlets in the hot butter and wondered how long to keep them on one side before turning them. "Have you ever made veal before?" she asked him.

"No. I've watched. You're doing fine from what I can tell."

After a few minutes, she turned them over, then looked at the recipe again to consult what to do next although she had read it several times already. "'Cook until done' doesn't help that much. Maybe another five minutes. They won't be raw at least."

Brendan shrugged. "I guess we'll find out. My culinary skills consist of making toast, scrambled eggs and coffee. The end."

"Somehow I feel we should have had this discussion about who would be the cook early in our relationship," she said.

"I had hoped I would be eating at the Burnside Manse forever. Cook is one of a kind."

"You might not believe this, but Rob has the chef from the Oasis deliver a meal every late afternoon to Louisa. Fully cooked! All she has to do is plop a sprig of parsley on the plate and ta-da!"

"Sadly, I don't own a nightclub."

"Well, we'll have to muddle through or go out to eat each night, which will get expensive."

"We'll figure it out," he said, pulling her toward him in an embrace and kissing her on the nose.

"While those are cooking, I have an interesting proposition to put forward."

"Uh-oh," he said, the usual comment when she was about to propose something.

"The Van Eaton property is for sale."

"Yes, I remember you mentioned it."

"And I think we can buy it."

"Wouldn't it seem ridiculous to be living in that huge place on a policeman's salary?"

"First, you're a detective at a lieutenant's level and your salary is quite nice. Second, I bring home a salary and commissions from private clients. And third, my trust fund money is sitting there waiting to be claimed. It can easily pay for the down payment, according to Spencer Whiting."

"Who is he?"

"Bitsy's husband. Louisa's old friend. He's a real estate broker and has what he calls the listing on it. We don't have to buy it outright, and we don't have the money for that anyway. But we can get a long-term mortgage and the rates are decent now at four percent."

"My savings account only pays one percent!" he said. "How can we possibly afford it?"

"Wait. Here's my idea. You've seen the layout of the property. Hugh Van Eaton rented out the bedrooms in the main house and lived in the separate place to the back."

"The servants' quarters?" he asked.

"I don't know who lived there originally, but it certainly is quieter away from the main street and private. It's much larger than this place, no offense to you or your family. And the rent from the four tenants in the big house could cover most, perhaps all, of the mortgage payments. Four single women would jump at the chance to live in a safe neighborhood in a furnished room."

Brendan furrowed his brow. "Do you think a bank would lend us the money?"

"I don't know. We can ask. We're both working so that should speak in our favor."

"What are you thinking of charging for rent?"

She gave him a number.

"That's a bit high, don't you think?"

"The rooms are furnished and they'll have that large sitting room, dining room and kitchen."

"Hm," he muttered.

Amanda jumped up to look at the cutlets, which hadn't been cooking very long. She turned off the heat and took them out of the pan, hoping they weren't overdone. The canned peas that had been bubbling away in their liquid were ready and she served them onto two plates and took a bowl of applesauce from the refrigerator. The meal was accompanied by bread and butter.

They sat down and Brendan put on a happy face as he began to saw through the cutlet. "Very tender," he said.

Amanda cut a piece of meat and was surprised at her achievement.

"Thank you, Fanny Farmer," she said. "But you know, we could hire a cook for the Van Eaton place and provide dinner for the tenants, too. It would not only justify the rental price but relieve them of having to go out for dinner or make it for themselves, which could be a culinary mistake or fire disaster. We could take our meals with them, providing company for them and taking the burden of cooking off me," she concluded.

"I'm sure you will conquer the world of cooking just fine in time, but having a cook, if we can get someone half as good as your parents', would relieve you of that."

"Well, the meat turned out well, the peas are almost mush, the applesauce came out of a jar, but I can assure you that the rice pudding is top-notch."

Chapter 3

At the Worleys' house, Louisa was indeed taking a sprig of parsley and placing it on the serving platter of filet of sole that the chef had brought over. In a separate bowl were potatoes duchesse, artfully arranged and finished with a few minutes of broiling. She had put some cubes of cheese and crackers on a plate as an appetizer and waited for Rob to come down to dinner. Before they married, he had spent most of the day at the club, going in after noon to check on the night's setup and staying until closing. Now, he went to the club in the late morning and came home to have dinner with his wife before returning downtown.

"That looks lovely, Darling," Rob said, scanning the elegant meal.

"I do wish your mother would join us each night," she said. "After all, she's just next door."

"You know she enjoys her privacy and is being respectful of ours. She eats more simply that we do, as well. How was Amanda?"

"Just fine. We did a little tour of the museum and ran into Bitsy."

"Remind me, which one is she?"

"Tiny thing married to Spencer Whiting. Do you know him or of him?"

"I think he does real estate. He made a big splash a few years ago by having an opening of his office."

Louisa looked puzzled.

"As if a business office opening was a reason to have a party. It was strange. Of course, he had it catered and asked us to supply the beverages, bartender and waiters, so I'm not complaining. He may have actually started a new trend. Instead of the discreet letters to former clients and contacts or an announcement in the business pages of the **Globe**, he got more attention by having a big bash with everyone who was anyone enjoying themselves at a lavish do."

"That's very good to know! It sounds as if my idea of a Halloween costume party to show off his listing of the Williams house would be right up his alley."

"Interesting. Are the people you intend to invite the sort of people who might buy the home?"

"Well, I hope so. I had the idea of thirty people under thirty years of age. Maybe I'll have to expand the guest list to older, wealthier folks." Louisa frowned at her original notion spoiled by practicality. "I was hoping that those invited would rush to Monsieur Josef to get costumes made."

"Ah, so that's what you're thinking." He winked at her.

"Yes, but we'd maybe charge for the drinks or tickets and that money could go to charity. Oh, Rob, I haven't thought this out very well at all. And to be honest, I haven't even asked Spencer if he thought it was a good idea."

"I suppose that's going to be your first step," Rob said.

After Rob left for the club, Louisa considered her plan in more detail and, summoning her courage, called Bitsy at home.

"It was so nice to see you today and I have to say that hearing about the Williams house and my long admiration for it and Spencer's connection to it got the wheels turning." She was aware that her voice sounded overly bright so she toned down her excitement as she outlined her proposal.

"Let me interrupt you," Bitsy said. "I'm going to get Spencer on the line."

They must have had an extension in their home because shortly after, both she and her husband were on the line. Bitsy gave a brief outline of what they had been talking about.

"I think that's a terrific idea. But I think we need to do it in mid-October. We don't want to conflict with the actual Halloween holiday."

"Oh, good point, Spence. Some of the guests will have children and there will be parties and school events that could conflict."

"How many people do you think would comfortably be accommodated in the Williams house?" Louisa asked.

"It's a three-story house, as you probably know. We'll want to keep people on the main floor. There's a huge sitting room and a sizable adjacent dining room. It's rather overcrowded with heavy Victorian furniture at the moment, but I can get that moved out for the night to protect those pieces—as if anybody wants that sort of thing anymore—and to give us more space."

"Should we have a band?"

"But of course, and I know just the fellows to ask. And a bar, and some food. Bitsy, can you arrange for the refreshments?"

"Gosh, I've never put together a big event like that. Just dinner parties," she said, sounding hesitant. "But I've heard of a caterer who can do some creative presentations."

Louisa thought about Rob's club doing that but hesitated, thinking it would look like they were taking over the entire event. She'd let Bitsy carry the weight of the event; it was for Spencer's benefit, after all.

"What about Halloween games?" Louisa asked.

"That would be great fun!" Bitsy said. "Grown people acting like children."

After having suggested it, Louisa then racked her brain for what they had done at children's parties. "Pin the tail on the donkey? Bobbing for apples?"

"I'm sure we can be more creative than that," Spencer said. "Let's put the planning on hold for now and get together over the weekend to flesh it out a bit. We've got about a month to put it together and you've really got my head reeling."

They agreed to meet at the Whitings' home on Saturday morning and Louisa ended the conversation, feeling proud of her achievement, and rushed to get paper and pen to put some of her thoughts down before they left her.

First, she started a list of thirty people—actually fifteen couples—who would be important enough that the social pages of the newspapers would take notice. She would be sure to contact them to send a photographer out to take pictures during the event, but thinking more strategically, perhaps she could suggest that photos be taken of the costumes as they were being created. That would be a great boost to Monsieur Josef's ego and future clientele since she had noticed that his 'ladies,' as he called them, were aging and the younger women were not filling the ranks. They seemed to want to go department stores for their new frocks, something he found shocking but she understood all too well.

To begin with, the stores reacted quickly to what shoppers wanted in the realm of what was seen in magazines and movies, and items were affordable, as opposed to the bespoke industry that relied on the more straight-laced and familiar wishes of the older women who had the funds for made-to-order clothes. Try as he might, Monsieur Josef could not get some of his tried-and-true clientele to experiment with the latest trends. The other factor was that, as his regulars were getting older, they were going through 'the change' and their bodies were no longer the slim things in years gone by. He had to accommodate the styles for that. Worse, some of the women were getting frugal as they aged and decided that the gown they wore two years previously for the winter gala would suffice this time around.

Louisa's goal was getting more exposure for the salon and her designs, of course, and possibly building up a new crop of wealthy young women who wanted to have one-of-a-kind pieces. It was a lofty goal but Louisa thought that, between her energy and Bitsy's address book, they could find exactly the kind of people who would fit the bill. If the Williams house got attention and interest or even sold, so much the better.

Chapter 4

Louisa was a little concerned that her proposal about costumes might seem self-serving, so her remedy was to persuade Amanda to join her at Spencer Whiting's home for backup.

"Why do I feel as though I am here as a shield for whatever scheme you may be hatching?" Amanda said, a bit annoyed at having part of her weekend interrupted.

"You're coming along to provide legitimacy to my endeavor."

"I thought it was legitimate," Amanda said.

"Yes. All but the costume part. Do you think it was too forward of me to suggest that they use my employer—and by extension me—to provide costumes? Obviously, they won't be free."

"Maybe you could let them know how much they might cost and say you're giving a discount for this one occasion."

"Good idea. It's not as if we'll be using the most expensive fabrics after all, and the guests probably won't use the costumes ever again. I know the salon has a lot of remnants that can be repurposed. And for some reason, a ton of black fringe that somebody ordered back in the past. Every outfit will be fringed!"

"Even Caesar and Cleopatra?" Amanda asked.

"Interesting thought."

Amanda raised her eyebrows at what she imagined that costume would be like.

"Actually, Cleopatra's costume is the one of the easiest. Two rectangles of white cotton gathered at the shoulders and a belt of some kind."

"Didn't they wear elaborate wigs?"

"I'm sure there will be one female guest with a dark brown bob and bangs. It will stand in for a wig just fine."

"Don't forget the asp," Amanda said.

They pulled up to the Whiting house. It was exactly where one of the brokers of Hammond & Whiting should live and what his residence should look like: totally modern and sleek, as if it had come out of a magazine or contemporary movie. And that was just the outside that looked somewhat out of place in a neighborhood with more traditionally designed homes.

"Gosh, I had no idea," Louisa said, stunned at the bold look.

The façade was stark white, almost a whitewashed look, with a broad curving overhang highlighting the bright blue door and round porthole window beside it. Everything seemed to be stone or plaster with metal accents, including a large window overlooking the street with metal frames. Behind this main structure was another story to the back, with the same metal-framed windows. The only landscaping in the front consisted of trimmed boxwood hedges and served to make the house stand out even more.

"I wonder what the neighbors think of it?" Amanda said.

Bitsy answered the door with a broad smile and ushered them in. The interior was just as striking as the exterior, with high ceilings and low sofas that added to the illusion of being in an enormous space.

"It's amazing!" Louisa said, looking around. Everything seemed black, white or gray and added to the modern aesthetic. "No fussy furniture here."

"My parents were apoplectic when they first saw the drawings, not to mention the final design. I suppose they imagined that Grandmother's high-backed red velvet chair was going to have the place of honor."

She led them to a hallway and then back to Spencer's study, where he sat behind a large, low table that served as his desk.

"Ladies, so nice to see you!" He got up and shook hands with them both, his cheeks red as he smiled. He was a big man and looked like an aging fraternity boy with an abundance of social energy.

"Have you seen the Williams house lately?" he asked them. "Please, sit, sit." He sat down as well and turned a photograph around to show them the exterior. "Perfect for a Halloween party, don't you think?" He laughed and they joined in as they looked at the gloomy structure, partially obscured by large trees.

"It's huge inside although very little daylight comes through because of the trees. But we'll be there at night, so that's not a problem. I'll have my men move the furniture into one of the outbuildings or upstairs and you'll be shocked at how much square footage is there. Black walnut wooden trim throughout."

"Now you're sounding like a salesman," Bitsy said.

He laughed. "Can't help it. Would either of you be interested?"

"What? In buying it?" Louisa asked. "Rob and I have a perfectly wonderful house."

"Spencer, you know I have my hopes set on the Van Eaton place," Amanda said. "We expect to hear back from the bank any day now."

"I haven't forgotten, believe me."

"Louisa, why don't you iron out the details and I'll show Amanda the rest of the house," Bitsy said.

"Sure."

They walked back down the hallway towards the stairway to the upper floor.

"This is a spectacular place," Amanda said.

"Yes, everyone admires it, but it sometimes seems a bit empty or cold. Oh, I know this design is all the rage and Spencer assures me that the resale value is tremendous. He's all about business, you know." They mounted the stairs and got to a landing that gave a view of the spacious room below.

"The architect called this a split-level house, or something. The floors are not one on top of each other but offset. Here, what you might call the mezzanine, is a sitting room that I've taken over for my burgeoning sketch factory." She laughed and they went into a room outfitted as a bedroom but now more of a studio, with an easel and a slanted drawing table. Brushes stood upright on a nearby table and drawings were pinned to the curtains.

"Spencer absolutely forbade me from poking holes in the walls, so I have to pin them to the drapes. For now."

"I love the north-facing light," Amanda said. "It seems the older houses all have tall trees blocking the view and adding unnecessary shade, especially in the winter."

"We opted for a cleaner approach and, to be honest, both Spencer and the architect wanted the house to stand out, so they cleared out all the trees and brush except for the backyard. That way, there is a shady place to sit or entertain on a hot summer's day."

"Who was the architect?"

Bitsy sighed. "A lovely young man. He's moved on since then. Let's go to the upper story."

Up a short flight of steps was a more traditional layout of what appeared to be four bedrooms all in a row. Bitsy began at the left most.

"Guest bedroom number one. We put Spencer's parents here when they visit. At the other end of the hall from us." She giggled.

"Bedroom number two." It had a large window that overlooked the front portion of the house.

"That would make a nice nursery," Amanda said.

"Spencer is not interested in children." She turned to Amanda. "So he says. But I can promise you, if one were on the way, he would be thrilled. I'm still working on him." She managed a smile but Amanda could see that Bitsy was deadly serious.

"Bedroom number three. Each was designed with their own bathroom. Sharing is such an annoyance, don't you think?"

"Indeed," Amanda said although she had always shared a bathroom with her sister. And most homes still had only one bathroom, even with large families who had to accommodate one another. Brendan had told her that his family had only one for many years and what a traffic jam it was in the morning as everyone had a turn until his father had another built out for them. Still, with seven of them it must have taken great coordination and patience to cope with it. It was certainly a better situation than the older tenement housing that had been in Boston with no indoor facilities and shared outhouses behind the building even though Brendan told her some of those still existed.

The master bedroom was enormous, larger than any bedroom Amanda had ever seen. The bed had a tufted satin headboard, and two huge night tables with light fixtures embedded in the walls above. What was extraordinary was that it was fitted out as a suite with a sofa, chairs and a low table near the windows that faced the street as if it were not just a place to sleep but somewhere to spend the day reading or daydreaming.

"I have to show you the silliest thing that Spencer insisted upon," Bitsy said, leading Amanda to the bathroom. There were the usual fixtures and a bathtub, but along one wall was a tiled enclosure that had multiple shower heads. "He likes to be bombarded by hot water when he showers," she added with a laugh. "I can't use it—that's the end of my hairdo and I can never figure out where the water will hit me next."

"The only thing that has been disappointing is the reaction of the neighbors. They seemed shocked that we demolished the former house and horrified that we cut down the trees in the front yard. Why, one of the old biddies even came up to me and shook her finger in my face about what she called the abomination."

"That's dreadful."

"So, that's the grand tour. Let's see what mischief those two are getting up to."

By the time they reached the study, Louisa was already on her feet and about to leave. Spencer came out from behind the desk, his face still flushed.

"We've got it all figured out, don't we?"

"Yes, well, we'll be in touch about details," Louisa said, a smile plastered on her face.

"Thank you for the hospitality, Bitsy," Amanda said.

"We can find our way out, don't worry," Louisa said, walking quickly.

It wasn't until they got into the car that Amanda turned to her sister. "What was that all about?"

"Spencer made a pass at me."

"What?"

"I was sitting next to him and as he was showing me the blueprints of the house, he got closer and closer. Then, the knee made its way over to my leg and that's when I got up."

"What a creep!"

"And the smell of whiskey at close quarters accounts for those rosy cheeks. I'm not meeting with him one-on-one again."

"You don't have to. That's why Alexander Graham Bell invented the telephone."

Chapter 5

The next few weeks were a flurry of activity as Bitsy found that filling out the guest list was more difficult than she had imagined. She had let go of Louisa's notion of having people buy tickets—that seemed to put cold water on the invitation—even if she had mentioned the funds were going to charity. The reality is that she hadn't given the philanthropic part of the evening much thought and couldn't think of what organization to support. For the sake of simplicity, she dropped the idea of tickets and donations entirely.

Louisa had tackled the task of finalizing the costumes, which she created in pairs as planned, and spoke strongly about assigning costumes. At first, Amanda thought it seemed overbearing to instruct people what they would wear, but she soon came to see that, if left to their own devices, there was such indecision and hesitation that Louisa's direct approach worked best.

The sisters managed to squeeze in a lunch to discuss the progress of the event.

Louisa explained her thinking. "The trick is not to ask open-ended questions such as, 'who do you want to be?' The men especially become flustered. You offer a choice: we have the Indian chief and Princess pair or the Robin Hood and Marion left. Then they make the decision very easily. We take their general measurements and on to the next."

"That's brilliant."

"There are a lot of outfits to put together and we're racing against time. We've even had to hire someone from off the street practically to do the finishing touches. On top of that, Monsieur Josef comes up to the atelier and, by the look on his face, I can tell he thinks the entire idea is strange and that the costumes look tawdry."

"They're costumes. They're supposed to look flashy, fun and over the top."

"Exactly. This isn't the court of Louis the Fourteenth, for heaven's sake. He's also concerned that orders for the winter and holiday season will be coming in and his women will still be sewing black fringe on everything. Luckily, they can do most of the work with sewing machines rather than by hand, so it's going fast."

"Wait—what did you have in mind for Brendan and me? I forgot to ask."

"I think Wizard and Witch will suit you."

Amanda furrowed her brow. "He'll be pleased to be a wizard, but I'm not so sure about the witch role. Do I have to have horrible hair and a wart on my chin?"

"We had a few black silk robes in the back room, so all we need to do is create a conical hat for Brendan with some sprinkles of stars and moons on it and a pointy black hat for you. You can be a young and flirty witch, not a crone."

"Thank you. I think adding the black fringe will make me look more flirty."

"Spencer wanted me to do a walkthrough of the house. I don't know why, but rather than be chased around that place by him, I told him I trusted his decisions completely."

"Speaking of Spencer, we had the closing on the Van Eaton house yesterday."

"That's wonderful!"

"The strange thing was that his charming demeanor often slips. He was back in his office and we were in the waiting room and an assistant went in with some paperwork. Spencer yelled at the poor fellow and called him an idiot. Then he emerged a few minutes later, all smiles and charming for us," Amanda said.

"That doesn't sound good. Maybe he's under a lot of pressure. I get the impression that he not only overspent on that immense house in which they live, but his office is in the most prestigious building in downtown Boston."

"The furnishings are over the top, in my opinion. No wooden chairs in that place. Luxurious leather armchairs, Persian rugs in every room—well, every room that I saw. I think Spencer has a Tiffany lamp on his desk," Amanda said.

"But the closing went well?"

"I'm excited and terrified at the same time. It's a huge step. But I've already heard from friends of friends of two young women who are looking for a rental in a nice neighborhood."

"You could be like a housemother," Louisa said with a chuckle.

"I am not going to get involved in the daily drama of their lives. As long as they're not leaving the lights on all day and night and increasing the electricity bill or letting the bathtub run over and wasting water, they are on their own."

"We'll see how that works out," Louisa said.

"Actually, I had the idea of providing a cook for evening meals."

"Like a boarding house?" Louisa asked, almost shocked.

"Think of it this way: if you were renting a room away from home in an entirely residential area, what would you do for dinner each night? Take a bus back downtown? Make it yourself? Eat ham and cheese sandwiches every day? Tuna out of a can? I'm more afraid of them messing around with the stove and oven. These girls have probably never cooked for themselves. And a cook would justify the rental price. That and the fact that the rooms are fully furnished."

"That makes perfect sense. One thing I've learned from working for Monsieur Josef is that, if you put a high price on something you are offering, the customer will value it even more."

"I like that. The bonus would be that I wouldn't have to cook. We could take our meals with them."

"Would you want to?"

"It might be fun. And if it isn't, we'll make a change."

"If I were a renter in such a situation, I don't know if I would want a man eating with us every night."

"Why? Do you think it would stifle conversation? Or would it have a civilizing effect? They could hardly come down to dinner in a wrapper or robe if there was a male present."

"Now you really are sounding like a housemother."

"Besides, we'll be at the Hallorans' for Sunday dinner and back at Mother and Daddy's on Wednesday evenings. We'll be giving the girls enough space while keeping an eye on things. Such as male visitors in the sitting room downstairs only. No sleepovers. I imagine that some parents might think more positively about their daughter living away from home if she's in an environment with other nice young ladies in a good neighborhood with a respectable married woman overseeing their well-being."

"And a seasoned police officer on site."

"Detective, Louisa. Lieutenant as well."

Louisa gave her sister a little salute. "When are you moving out of your current place?"

"Soon enough. Bit by bit. I still haven't totally moved out of our Beacon Hill house."

"Ugh, don't mention it. My closet back home is still stuffed. It might be time to give some of that away."

"You do have an impressive collection of evening wear. I'm sure it would take you a few weeks to rotate through them all," Amanda said.

"Except that some are outdated."

"Already! You made most of them in the past two years!"

"Time marches on," Louisa said. "I can't wear last year's designs—what sort of advertisement would that be for Monsieur Josef? And I must look particularly glamorous as the wife of the most prominent club owner in Boston."

Amanda raised her eyebrows. "Well, sister, I am glad I don't have your problems."

Chapter 6

The day of the party was soon upon them and Louisa had the good sense to allow Spencer and his beleaguered assistant to oversee the details. With one caveat: only she knew who would be wearing which costumes. It had been agreed early on that every guest would be given a black mask with the idea that, at some time towards the end of the evening, there would be a big reveal.

Rob and Louisa as King and Queen had agreed to meet Brendan and Amanda as Wizard and Witch at the Burnsides' home prior to going to the party.

"I feel a bit ridiculous walking around in the street like this," Brendan said, removing his wizard's hat and looking around in the dark street in front of the Burnsides' Beacon Hill home to see if anyone had noticed this strange attire.

"Put it back on inside. My parents will get a kick out of our costumes."

He scowled.

"I can see Rob and Louisa are already here," she commented, noticing their car parked out on the street in front of the house.

When they entered the sitting room, Mrs. Burnside clapped her hands together with excitement.

"Oh, just look at you!"

"Sorry, I left my broom in the car," Amanda said, twirling around.

"Can I take my hat off now?" Brendan asked, tucking his wand under his arm.

"I think you've suffered enough," she said.

"Oh, come now. Be a good sport," Louisa said.

"That's easy for you to say, decked out as a queen. Nobody is going to laugh at you and Rob."

"You haven't seen some of the other costumes," Louisa said. "I've got someone decked out as the Wolf who is coming with Little Red Riding Hood."

"You look quite wise and impressive," Rob said seriously. "It's an entirely appropriate outfit for you."

"Thank you, my good man. I'll be sure to ward off any evil spells sent your way."

"That's the spirit."

"Come have a glass of champagne that Rob brought," Mr. Burnside said. He began to wrestle with the cork before Rob subtly suggested that he step in. And with a twist and a slight pop, the top was off. Louisa held out a coupe glass to be filled, passing it to her mother. When all the glasses were full, Mr. Burnside held his up to make a toast.

"To your successful party." He nodded at Louisa and Rob. "And to our new neighbors in Beacon Hill!" He nodded this time toward Brendan and Amanda.

Thanks were given and the first sips taken before everyone sat down.

"You might be thankful as the night goes on that you have such a comfortable costume," Louisa said to Brendan. "I know some of the folks might complain. But luckily, I, too, will be wearing a mask so they won't know who to grumble to."

"I'll have to agree with you on that. The worst costume would be a tight collar, tie and modern suit," Brendan said. "The kind we men have to wear every day."

"I'LL BET our Julius Caesar thinks he got off easily, but while walking around in a toga is fine, holding the mantle in place takes practice. I can't imagine what he'll look like trying to dance."

The three couples finished their drinks and the two in costumes stood up.

"I was about to ask when you were coming home tonight," Mrs. Burnside said. Instead of her eyes welling with tears, she was able to laugh at herself.

They bade goodnight and drove in separate cars to the party house, which was visible as they approached due to floodlights illuminating the façade.

"That doesn't look much like a haunted house now," Amanda said. "I've never been inside. It was always an object of some fear when we were children. I hope we'll have some time to explore before the other guests arrive."

The front door was opened by a young man who nodded to them.

"Greetings, my name is Reggie." He gestured for them to come in and go to their right, where they found themselves in what was once a vast sitting room now cleared of furniture for dancing. Lamps had been placed on the floor at equal distances on one side, highlighting the high ceiling. On the other side of the room was a musician seated at a piano playing softly while a bass player thumped a beat.

Through an archway into the dining room, a large table covered in hors d'oeuvres had been positioned against the windows; on the other side of the room a makeshift bar had been set up with the room's shelves holding bottles of alcohol. The rest of the room was ringed with what must have been the previous owner's dining room chairs.

"Hello," Louisa said to the young man behind the bar. "This is Randy, Spencer's assistant. This is my husband Rob, my sister Amanda and her husband Brendan. Where are Spencer and Bitsy?"

"They've just stepped into the kitchen to give the servers some directions."

"Oops, we forgot to put our masks on," Louisa said. At that, she took one out of her purse and the other three reluctantly put theirs on.

"Do we really have to wear these things all night?" Brendan asked.

"Nobody knows who we are now except Randy. I guess

we'll have to kill him so as not to tell our secret," Louisa said.

Randy gave a wan smile and rearranged the glasses. "Could I interest you in a drink?"

"Put a little enthusiasm into it, Randy!" Spencer shouted as he pushed through the swinging door to the kitchen. He was followed by a photographer with a large camera pointed their way.

"Hold that pose!" he said.

Randy took a deep breath, put a smile on his face and cocked his head at the four guests as if he had just repeated the request.

The bulb flashed, sizzled and popped onto the floor. The two couples were momentarily blinded by the light and tried to blink it away. But they made their drink orders and greeted Spencer, dressed as a cowboy with what appeared to be uncomfortably tight boots.

"Blast—I forgot to put my mask on," he said. "Bitsy!" he yelled, turning toward the kitchen. "Masks!"

She emerged dressed as a cowgirl in a tan shirt and skirt, fringed in black.

Recognizing the embellishment as one that was on her costume as well, Amanda had to smile at Louisa's ingenuity.

"Hello, whoever you are," Bitsy said, knowing full well who the King and Queen were and making a good guess as to the couple with them.

"Hocus-pocus." Brendan waved his wand in her direction and his deadpan delivery had them all laughing.

"I've got a wonderful roster of games that we can play, and, of course, we'll have dancing. Are we ready for Halloween?"

They all cheered in agreement.

"Hold that pose!" the photographer said after reloading a fresh bulb. "Can I get your names?"

"Sorry, top secret for now," Brendan said, glad to escape the scrutiny.

AMANDA AND BRENDAN didn't get to explore the rest of the house because less than a half hour later, the two rooms were full of guests who spanned centuries and continents by way of their costumes. The young man stationed at the door was equipped with extra masks to hand out to those who either forgot or purposefully neglected to put one on. If they were annoyed at having to follow the protocol, once inside they saw everyone except the bartender, servers and the band were similarly accessorized. Each guest was given a small booklet like a dance card with a list of the costumed personages with a blank line next to it and a pencil on a string.

Amanda congratulated Louisa on the detail in the costuming, especially the historic ones, and the simplicity of others. For example, Cleopatra's was a simple floor-length tunic, cinched at the waist, but the addition of sandals made the costume look authentic.

Bitsy stood by the piano while the musician executed a fanfare and she clapped her hands for attention.

"Good evening, everyone. We have games and prizes to give out." There were cheers. "Your costumes have been assigned by me and Louisa and no one else knows who is who. Your job is to correctly guess who is impersonating each character. The person with the most correct guesses will receive the grand prize."

"What's that?" someone shouted.

"That is another secret you will have to discover."

She waved her hand and the band began to play.

"Well, we know two couples already," Brendan said. "I guess our task is to try to have conversations with others to figure out who they might be."

"You're a natural at that, Brendan," Amanda said.

"I might be, but these are more likely people you already know. So, *you* are the best one to set the trap."

After the band's first short set, Bitsy clapped her hands. "Who is up for bobbing for apples? This way, please."

Amanda followed into an adjoining room and, seeing that the apples were small, decided she might be able to be successful. She removed her hat and stood at the rim of the large, galvanized tub filled with water and waited for the other contestants to line up.

"What does the winner get?" she asked.

"Candy," Bitsy said, holding up a decorated bag. Everyone whooped and others came closer to watch.

"Most unsanitary," said a voice behind her that she instantly recognized as her ex-boyfriend, Fred Browne, who was physician. She turned to look at his costume, a remarkable take on Napoleon, complete with a bicorne hat. Standing in front of him and next to her was Josephine—actually her friend Valerie—in a charming black-and-white Empire waist gown trimmed in the ubiquitous black fringe.

"Everybody ready? Hands behind your back," Bitsy called out. "Begin!"

There was quite a bit of splashing even though it was only the faces that were in the water, and Amanda wondered if her mascara would run before deciding that it would add authenticity to her costume. A large fellow dressed as the Sun pulled his head up and took the apple from his mouth.

"No fair! He grabbed the smallest fruit," someone said.

"Here's your prize. Now back to dancing."

Amanda made her way to the cloakroom to retrieve her purse and comb out her wet hair. Looking in her compact, she saw minimal damage to her makeup and none to her hair since it was in a straight bob and never had any curl to it. Patched up with a touch of powder and lipstick, she went back to find her Wizard and join in a dance.

"I just found out Fred and Valerie are Napoleon and Josephine," she said.

"Good work! What do you imagine the grand prize is?"

"The apple bobbing was a bag of candy, so don't get your hopes up for anything significant."

"Don't forget I have a magic wand and can make anything happen."

"Do be quiet and let's dance."

After the band's next set, Spencer made an announcement. "Folks! I've invited you here for a party but also to see this magnificent house." Everyone had guessed who the cowboy and cowgirl were already. "Follow me," he called out and everyone trooped after him up the stairs to the second floor.

"Mind that some of the rooms are filled with furniture we moved from downstairs to make space for the dancing but look at all the space." He turned on the overhead light to reveal an enormous room with a billiard table in the middle and racks of cues along the wall. "Wouldn't this be a swell party room," he said. The group walked around behind him as he circled the table, pausing in the doorway to allow others in before going to the next room.

"A study," he declared in his booming voice. "There's a library downstairs but plenty of books here, too."

One wall was bookshelves fully stocked. The other furniture in the room was a desk, armchairs and a couch.

"Do they come with the house?" someone asked.

"Everything must go—so why not? Just look at those windows," Spencer said. It was more of a squeeze for him and the others to move around the furniture before they followed him down the hall to a bedroom, where he stopped at the door.

"Bedroom with the sitting room's furniture," he said, turning on the overhead light but not venturing in as there was little room. "There is a huge walk-in cedar closet to keep the moths at bay."

The next few rooms looked the same—piled high with furniture. They came to the end of the hallway. "Servants' quarters upstairs, full attic, full basement, a separate garage, all on an acre."

There was murmuring and he shepherded them back the way they had come, turning off the lights in the rooms as he went. He stopped outside the billiard room and gestured for them to precede him down the stairway before he turned off that light.

"Now even with my mask on, you know who I am. You know how to get in touch with me and I guarantee a fair price for this beautiful, one-of-a-kind mansion. I know that one of you is dying to purchase it."

Chapter 7

The band began to play again and the guests refreshed their drinks while others wandered into the dining room to get something to eat. Amanda was amused by the carefully thought-out Halloween-themed selections: stuffed eggs made to look like eyeballs, peeled tangerines with celery stick stems to resemble pumpkins, gingerbread, finger sandwiches, nuts, grapes and bite-sized, orange-colored popcorn balls. Amanda was impressed by the organization it took to put the event together.

After a while, the music stopped and Bitsy stepped forward again. "Another game! Charades!" Everyone clapped as that was a familiar and enjoyable parlor game. "A prize to the person or couple who guesses correctly." Spencer was the one to act out the clue and began in the familiar way of indicating it was a movie by imitating someone winding a camera.

"Movie!" someone shouted.

With his fingers, Spencer tapped four times on his forearm.

"Four words," the group said in unison.

Spencer crossed his arms and moved them back and forth.

"Rocking!"

"What movie is that?" someone asked with a laugh.

"Babes in Toyland!"

Spencer shook his head and repeated the motion.

"Baby," someone called out.

He nodded. Then he held out his hand as if to snatch something.

"Grabs!"

"Angry!"

Spencer repeated the motion.

"Take! Takes! Baby Takes a Bow!" Maid Marion said and hugged her partner, Robin Hood. It was a popular Shirley Temple movie.

"Another bag of candy," Bitsy said, producing it and handing it to the winners.

"Darn, I know I've heard that voice, but I can't figure out who she is," Amanda said about Maid Marion.

"Next," Bitsy announced, handing her husband a piece of paper.

The paper went into his pocket and he held his hands side by side in an open gesture.

"Book!" someone said.

He tapped twice on his arm.

"Two words!"

Spencer looked around and everyone assumed he was looking for something.

"Searchers!" someone called out.

"What book is that?" someone else said.

"Looking!"

Spencer shook his head. He then mimed putting his hand over his eyes and turning his head from side to side.

"Searching!" the same voice said.

"Looking Backward!" someone said.

That was greeted by another voice, "What book is that?"

Spencer gazed down at the ground and around his feet.

"Looking for…" the voice trailed off.

"Lost! Lost Horizon!"

Applause and groans were equally heard from the group.

"Your reward," Bitsy said, handing it to the couple who had won.

"Ha!" said Amanda. "I know that voice. That's Lorna, one of Louisa's old friends. We're making headway on the grand prize," she said as she thought she had identified the Devil and Angel.

The music started up again and many couples retired to the dance floor while others replenished their drinks. Louisa and Rob approached and asked Amanda and Brendan what they thought of the party.

"It's lots of fun so far, but that wasn't much of a sales pitch if he thinks anyone here is going to buy it," Amanda said.

"The publicity may help some, but I'm sure he'll write off all he's spent tonight, including his costume, as business expense," Rob said.

"I see that I must be in the wrong profession," Brendan said.

"Let me see your card," Louisa said to her sister. "My goodness, you've filled in quite a few names."

"How close am I?"

"My lips are sealed," Louisa said since she knew exactly who everyone was.

"I'm pretty sure that George Washington is José Guzmán," Amanda said.

"How in the world can you tell with that powdered wig, much less the mask?" Brendan asked.

"The shoes."

Everyone looked over at the colonial President and First Lady and recognized a modern and very expensive set of brogues.

"Very good!" Louisa said. "Anyone would think you were a private investigator."

"Also, he seems like a fish out of water when it comes to these silly games."

"You don't think they have Charades where he came from?" Brendan asked.

"They must. He just doesn't get the American references."

The music stopped and Bitsy stepped in front of the piano. "I've got another game!"

There was some clapping and a few groans.

"Not everyone has to take part. We just need two teams of four." She waited while eight people stepped forward. "One of you is going to be the mummy. And the others have to wrap you up."

The participants looked puzzled.

"Here are the wrappings." Bitsy held up two large rolls of white crepe paper. The eight folks shrugged at how easy a task that would be.

"You may begin," she said and threw the rolls out so that the paper entirely unrolled.

Everyone laughed except the participants who scrambled to find an end and raced back to their designated mummy. It was a confused effort as the two teams got tangled up and Julius Caesar tripped on his robe. After what seemed like an eternity, one team shouted that they had won.

"Here's your prize," Bitsy said holding up a bag of candy in front of the winners' mummy who obviously couldn't take it since his hands were bound to his sides.

"Get me out of here!" Peter Pan shouted, wiggling his fingers and pulling his hand free. His teammates, including Wendy, a Policeman and Robber, had great fun unwinding him as he tore at the crepe paper to get to his prize.

Bitsy took Spencer aside for a moment to suggest that the newspaper's photographer had enough shots for the evening and was giving everyone a headache with the flashes. With an arm around the man's shoulder, Spencer escorted the man to the front door.

"Now, while everyone is in a jolly mood, I propose a game of sardines," Bitsy said after she heard the door close.

Everyone clapped at the idea except George Washington, who shrugged his shoulders and held out his hands in confusion toward Martha.

"See, I told you. It's José," Amanda said.

"Everyone into the dining room, please. Get your drinks and something to eat while I go hide." Seeing the first President's befuddlement, she outlined the rules. "Whoever finds me joins me and everyone else one by one does too. Now turn around—no peeking—count down very slowly to one hundred," she added.

"Nobody in the basement, please," Spencer added, shooing the guests forward into the dining room while Bitsy disappeared. "Who wants to do the counting?" he shouted. "One, two…I'll have a glass of whiskey, Randy," he said to the bartender and, taking it neat, disappeared into the kitchen. The four servers came out and wove through the loud crowd with small trays, picking up used dishes and glasses. As the guests continued counting, they became louder and louder, which got in the way of ordering drinks or getting a bite to eat.

"Are we really going to do this?" Brendan asked. "I stopped playing this game when I was eight years old."

"Poor boy, you grew up too fast. You know these folks, they'd do anything to be silly, as you've witnessed," Louisa said.

"I don't relish crashing around in the dark," Rob said. "I believe I'll sit this one out."

"Good idea," Brendan said with relief, finding a chair alongside the wall and sitting down. Rob joined him while their wives shook their heads at their husbands' reluctance.

"They just don't want to look foolish," Amanda said.

"One hundred!" someone concluded, and anyone who was not in the middle of eating something moved into the empty sitting room.

"Did she go up the stairs?" Someone asked the piano player, who shrugged.

"There are probably back stairs," another said. "But you'd get to them through the kitchen and she'd have to go through the dining room. We would have seen her. I think she went upstairs."

"Maybe she went out the front door," someone suggested, opening it and peering out into the chilly night. "Maybe not."

The group slowly fanned out, some looking behind curtains in the unused but furnished rooms downstairs while others opened closets and cupboards.

Amanda and Louisa went upstairs, along with many others who were busy chatting and casually peering under the billiard table or opening a closet door.

"Spencer said for nobody to go into the basement but he didn't say anything about the attic. Or the servants' rooms on the third floor," Louisa said. "Let's go on up." They went further than Spencer's original tour had taken them and found that one door at the end of the hall on the second floor was not a closet, but a set of stairs up to the next story.

"Is it cheating to turn on a light?" Amanda asked. "I don't want to break my neck stumbling around in the dark."

"Of course not." Louisa felt along the wall and located a switch that illuminated the steep staircase with a dim bulb and they ascended.

"Gosh, it's freezing and it smells as if nobody has been up here in ages," Amanda said.

"Maybe we'll be able to see footprints in the dust."

"I really wish I had brought a flashlight with me. I knew she was going to play this game, but I was too preoccupied with everything else."

They heard a noise and stopped to look at one another in the gloom.

"What was that? Bitsy?" Louisa called out.

"I don't think it's fair play to find her by calling her name."

They stood still for a moment, heard another noise and then, out of the dark, a large orange cat raced past them and down the stairs. They both screamed in alarm before dissolving into laughter.

"Oh, we are such brave gals, aren't we?" Amanda said.

"Who's that?" a voice called out from behind them at the base of the stairs.

"We're not Bitsy. Just getting spooked by noises in the dark."

"What's up there?"

"We're about to find out."

Whoever had initiated that brief conversation closed the door, so the sisters continued up and felt for another light switch at the top of the stairs. It illuminated a long hall with many doors for what must have been the large staff of the former owner.

"Do you think she came up this far?" Louisa asked, reluctant to search every room.

"We'll never know until we look, will we? Why don't you take one side and I'll take the other. Don't forget to look under the bed and in the closet."

The first room Amanda entered was small and sparsely furnished with a single bed, small night table and lamp, and chest of drawers with a mirror above. The closet smelled of moth balls. One sash window was the only natural light and the view must have been of the back of the house because there was no lighting, unlike the floodlights in the front.

Amanda went on to the next without finding anything but certain that she heard the scratching noise of a mouse in quick retreat. When she went to the next room, she heard Louisa give a yelp from across the hall. She ran to the room whose door was open.

"What is it?"

Louisa stood with her hand over her mouth and gestured to the form on top of the metal bedsprings. Amanda turned on the overhead light and approached.

"It's just the mattress rolled up. Not a body."

"I don't want to do this alone," Louisa said.

Amanda sighed. "Fine, we'll go together. Have you looked in the closet yet?"

"No," Louisa said but made no move to do so.

"Honestly," Amanda said, opening the door and seeing nothing but two empty hangers on the rod. "Let's finish my side," she said and opened the third door to see that it was a bathroom with nobody in it. Two more bedrooms did not reveal Bitsy or anything else of interest. The other side had the same sad-looking empty rooms and another bathroom.

"Do you think she's in the attic?" Louisa asked.

"I'm not going to check. Let's go down to the second floor and see what's happening there."

As they reached the bottom of the stairs and opened the door, there was a buzz of quiet conversation that quickly stopped.

"I bet she's here," Louisa said. She tiptoed down the hallway and stopped to listen. "They're in here," she said, opening the door to one of the bedrooms that was piled high with furniture. "I know you're in here, Bitsy," she said.

There was a snort and a giggle. Louisa walked around the clump and saw that there was a drop cloth over much of it. She tugged it aside. "Aha!"

"Shh," said Bitsy and the other people in unison.

"How are we to cram ourselves in here?"

"There's actually plenty of room if Cleopatra would move over a bit," Holmes said, glancing over to the Queen of the Nile. Amanda watched as she tucked her bare feet under her white drapery and slid back a bit.

"I'm sorry, I'm taking off this blasted mask," Holmes continued. "I can hardly see where I'm going anyway."

"Shh," Watson said. "Someone is coming."

The footsteps stopped at the doorway. "I already checked in here when we first started. She's not in here," a woman's voice said.

"Well, check again," said a man.

The footsteps halted as the woman lifted one end of the drop cloth and peered under, but all the sardines were squashed up against a piece of furniture that hid them from view. The man's footsteps moved on in the hall but the woman had tiptoed further into the room, picked up the cloth and said, "Aha! Got you, you miserable little fishes! But you weren't here before."

"Yes, I was," Bitsy said. "I was ever so quiet when you came in earlier and I was still the only one."

"Well, make room, folks," the woman said. Even in the dim light she could see that two people no longer wore masks. "Can we take these off now?"

"That wasn't the intention."

"Well, it's ruining my makeup, I'm sure," Little Red Riding Hood said, pulling it off.

"Aren't you a little young to be wearing makeup?" Bitsy said.

"I like them young," the Wolf replied with a leer.

"Oh, be quiet, George," his wife said.

They were quiet and it was strange to be smashed up in close quarters in an old house with a bunch of adults.

Amanda could catch the familiar scent of Louisa's Chanel Number 5 as well as some strong jasmine perfume, and she wondered how much longer they would have to stay there in awkward silence.

A few people came up to the open doorway and stopped, murmured something and moved on.

"Is there an end to this game?" Watson asked. "It's getting a bit stuffy in here."

They sat for a few more minutes in silence until they heard a scream.

"So, you think they were attacked by the cat as we were?" Louisa asked.

"He didn't attack us. He was probably more startled by our presence," Amanda said.

There was another scream and then a lot of people were running down the hall and the stairs.

"Something is the matter, Bitsy," Amanda said. "Maybe someone fell in the dark."

They scrambled out from under the cover, brushed themselves off from the dust of the floor and then picked up speed to find out where the screams had come from.

George was first down the stairs, the tail of his Wolf's costume flailing back and forth as he took the steps two at a time.

"What's going on?" he shouted.

They had arrived at the bottom of the stairs and, proceeding through the sitting room into the dining room, found the door to the kitchen was open. Swarming into the kitchen with the others, George repeated, "What's going on?"

Rob, who was at the back of the kitchen at the head of the stairs to the basement, had his arm around one of the servers, who was quivering in fear.

"It's Spencer. He seems to have fallen down the stairs."

Chapter 8

"It can't be!" Bitsy said, pushing to the front of the crowd. "He specifically said no one was to go to the basement." She looked past Rob and the girl and pushed them out of the way to clamber down the steps. "Spencer! What are you doing?" She shook him and screamed. "He's dead!"

There was utter silence for a few moments before others went into action. Rob removed the young woman who had discovered their host and who still stood near the open basement door, transfixed by the scene. Brendan went down the stairs and escorted Bitsy back to the kitchen. Then taking off his mask and hat, he went back down the steps to check on Spencer's condition. He came back up slowly.

Bitsy was seated at one of the chairs at the enamel table in the kitchen, staring into space.

"I'm sorry. I'm afraid he's gone," Brendan said.

There was a terrible hush in the room although everyone was aware that the other guests had gathered in the dining room after hearing the commotion and had crowded toward the swinging door to overhear what was going on.

"He can't be. He said nobody was to go into the basement. Why would he have done that?" she asked. "I told him not to wear those stupid cowboy boots. He could barely walk in them."

She stopped speaking, realizing how absurd her comments were.

"Somebody get her a brandy," was heard from the back of the crowd and shortly thereafter, Randy, the erstwhile bartender for the night, appeared with a glass. Bitsy stared at it as if she had never seen a glass before.

She stood, glanced around, and fell over in a faint.

Several women came to the rescue, loosening her blouse, patting her hands and trying to revive her. Fred Browne came through the crowd and asked everyone to step aside as he would deal with the situation. He stretched Bitsy's arms and legs out and then gently turned her to the side and felt in her mouth for any obstruction.

"Do you have any vinegar?" he asked, expecting one of the servers to respond.

As they had been hired for the evening and were unfamiliar with the house, they rapidly opened and closed cabinets before they found a bottle and handed it to the doctor. He opened it and put it under Bitsy's nose, to which she had the expected reaction of twisting her head away and groaning.

"Stay down," he told her. "Could somebody get a pillow or cushion or towel?"

A kitchen towel was produced and he folded it and gently placed it under her head. Her eyelids flickered open and she tried to get up.

"Not just yet," he said and she relaxed.

Brendan ushered everyone out of the kitchen and asked them not to leave the house. By then, everyone had removed their mask and many took that opportunity to go to the bar and get another drink.

"Fred, could you take a look at Spencer? We have, but we need a professional assessment."

Fred got up and went down the stairs while Amanda and Louisa knelt next to Bitsy on the kitchen floor. He came back up shortly thereafter and shook his head.

"What was he doing down there after warning everyone else away?" Brendan said.

"I don't know," Bitsy said.

"I'm sorry, I wasn't questioning you—just thinking aloud." He turned to see an old-fashioned telephone on the kitchen wall and picked up the earpiece and was surprised to hear a dial tone. He dialed the station and quietly asked for assistance.

"I want to get up," Bitsy said. "I can sit in a chair."

She was assisted into the kitchen chair she had abandoned previously and took a big gulp of the brandy.

"This isn't real," she said in a monotone.

Brendan went through the swinging door into the dining room where everyone stood or sat in silence.

"We're going to be here for a while so make yourselves comfortable. "I think there are enough chairs here and more in the library."

Amanda looked around and noticed that her guesses at identifications were correct for the most part. The exceptions were the Angel and the Devil, not two of Louisa's friends, but the man's moustache and short, pointed beard were positively diabolical.

"What happened?" someone asked.

"Spencer seems to have fallen down the steps. I'm afraid he's dead."

There was a gasp from several people who were at the entrance to the kitchen and didn't know the outcome.

"I'm Brendan Halloran, Chief Detective Boston Police and I've called for assistance. It might just have been an accident, but it's important that we talk to everyone to ascertain why he might have gone down to the basement, especially after warning everyone else off."

"How long will we be here?" someone asked.

"We need to get names and contact information for preliminary statements. Other detectives are coming to assist," he said. He realized that he didn't have paper, pencil or pen with him and went off in search of that in the rooms on the first floor that had been previously blocked off. Down the end of one hall was the library with a leather-topped desk and an open book that looked as if someone had just got up and walked away. Opening the desk, he found the former owner's stationery and pencils, although he would have preferred his own fountain pen that he had left in his car. This would have to do.

Brendan looked down at his costume and promptly took it off. Underneath he had worn suit pants, shirt and tie, so he didn't look so ridiculous, but he wished he had a jacket. Remembering that he was going to be getting statements from people in more absurd outfits, he collected himself and went back out to the dining room. Looking around, he called the kitchen staff into the adjacent sitting room but out of sight and hearing of the guests.

"Were any of you in the kitchen when Mr. Whiting came in and went down the stairs?"

"No, I mean yes," said one young woman. "He came in the kitchen and asked all of us to go into the dining room and see if used plates or glasses needed to be brought back into the kitchen. It was so noisy as they were counting down for the game they were playing. We certainly didn't see him go down the stairs. We took note of what items were running low before coming back into the kitchen. Then Connie here noticed the door to the basement was ajar and she went to shut it and the light from the kitchen showed something at the bottom."

"And then I saw him. It was Mr. Whiting," Connie said.

"Do you all work for the Whiting family?"

"We two do," said the other young woman. "But the other two girls were hired for the night."

Brendan's brain was buzzing with the enormity of so many people who were present, all of whom would have to be interviewed to rule out any foul play. He glanced at his watch to see that it was half past eleven. Perhaps when the other detectives arrived, they could do some preliminary sorting of those present and get initial impressions and then do follow-up interviews in the coming days.

It was some time before Dominic Barone and Clyde Owens showed up, both looking as if they had been dragged from their beds.

"Gentlemen, this way," Brendan said, leading them through the dining room where they gaped at the costumed guests who sat solemnly in chairs around the room.

They pushed through the swinging door to the kitchen and Brendan led them to the door to the basement. Clyde went down first and being effectively the head of the forensic team, he trod delicately for someone so large in order not to disturb any possible evidence. He had brought a flashlight to see more than what the dim bulb illuminated. He poked around and looked at Spencer's boots with interest before coming back up.

"It's a wonder he didn't fall down the stairs in those ridiculous, pointy boots with the high heels."

"His was a cowboy costume," Brendan clarified.

"Even so. The boots are made for keeping your feet in the stirrups, not walking around. You've seen how cowboys look in movies when they walk. As if their feet are killing them."

He demonstrated for their benefit.

"I never noticed," Dominic said, blinking sleep from his eyes and wondering why they were called out to listen to that absurd observation.

"It looks like he broke his neck," Clyde said.

"Yes, the doctor who was here as a guest confirmed as much. Perhaps those boots propelled him down the stairs,"

Brendan said. "But what he was doing going into the basement by himself is the question."

"Is this his house?" Dominic asked.

"No, he's a real estate broker and he's trying to sell this house. It was part of the plan, as far as I know, that he put on a flashy party and invited a newspaper photographer to take pictures in the hopes of stirring up interest."

"Not your typical starter home." Dominic said.

"It used to belong to the Williams family and I guess they're all gone," Brendan said. He saw that Clyde was anxious to say something.

"I'm afraid that Mr. Whiting may have slipped or tripped in his cowboy boots. But it didn't help that someone had rigged an impediment across the steps."

Brendan stared. "I didn't see anything. Show me."

"It was a wire. Not very sophisticated, but ample enough to trip him. It broke upon impact so you might not have seen the two ends fastened with eye screws."

The three detectives went back to the door to the basement and carefully down the stairs, Clyde leading the way and shining his flashlight on either side of the steps far above where the body lay.

"You're right. We were so focused on where he landed that we didn't look further up the steps for what might have been there. If we're careful, now, let's step around the late Mr. Whiting and explore further in the basement to see what he might have been here for."

Clyde first shone his light around the massive room that was almost empty except for a boiler and a drain pump in the event of water leakage into the room. At the far end was the usual coal room and the remainder of the room was dust. Overhead was an array of pipes and wires that supplied the rooms above.

"My family's basement has my father's workbench and tools. Obviously, this family didn't do their own home repairs," Dominic said.

"Why was he coming down here? There's nothing here. He'd been through the entire house many times and knew that. Was he meeting someone? Why down here? This house is huge. He could have met whomever it was in one of about twenty rooms, by my count," Brendan said.

"We'll be sure to ask the Medical Examiner to look and see if there are any defensive wounds. Let's be sure to check out the guests upstairs to see if any of them might have been in a scuffle. I don't want to touch the body before he sees it," Clyde said.

They climbed the stairs and were back in the kitchen. Dominic saw several doors and opened each one in turn. One that was unlocked led to the backyard, another to a small servant's bathroom, another led into the hallway and a fourth to the back stairs.

"I should have seen that," Brendan said. "It's likely whoever he was to meet came either down the back stairs or in from the hallway to do so. That's why he asked the staff to leave the room. Someone coming through the dining room could have been seen.

"Or maybe they came through the back door. Or they could have been hiding in the bathroom all along."

"We've got our work cut out for us."

Chapter 9

The guests were somber but also getting restless as the detectives got names and contact information from everyone. Louisa had brought a list of those who had been invited and that needed to be checked against who had actually showed up. The kitchen staff and Spencer's assistants supplied their information and were told that they would be contacted in the coming days to be interviewed.

"Did we miss anybody?" Brendan asked Amanda.

"Yes, the photographer. We can track him down at the newspaper."

"We'll need to take a look at those pictures and see if there is anything that can assist us."

The Medical Examiner, who never liked being called out late at night and certainly not on the weekend, arrived with a scowl on his face. It deepened when his eyes ran over the motley group of costumed adults and he shook his head. He was led to the head of the basement stairs and muttered when he saw the boots and the dim lighting.

While he manipulated Spencer's neck, he heard another set of footsteps in the kitchen that halted.

"The ambulance is here," Clyde called down to the doctor.

"Very well. I'm done here." He grunted as he stood up and brushed the dust off the knees of his pants. "What a stupid thing to do."

The loaded stretcher was brought back through the dining room and sitting room with the silent guests staring at the spectacle. They didn't move until the front door was closed; then some gulped down the remainder of drinks they held in their hands.

"You're free to go, but we'll be in touch," Brendan said.

"We'll take Bitsy back to my place," her brother, dressed as an old-fashioned police officer, said, and the once rollicking, silly party came to its solemn conclusion.

Brendan conferred briefly with Dominic and Clyde and they concluded that it made no sense to go back to the station at that late hour. The kitchen staff placed the perishable food in the refrigerator, wrapping up the rest and, once they were gone, Randy and the other assistant produced keys and locked up.

Brendan and Amanda didn't get home until after two o'clock.

"I'm more exhausted than I thought," she said, removing her costume. "What an awful night."

"Does Monsieur Josef want his costumes back?" Brendan asked. "I've lost my hat and wand."

"No, they were yours to lose. Everyone paid for their own costumes." She wondered why in the world he had asked such a strange question. Perhaps it was the late hour and the events.

"I'm going to have a heck of a week. Who would want to kill Spencer? All his best friends were at the party, wouldn't you say?" Brendan asked.

"Aren't those the first people you look at?" Amanda sat at her vanity table and applied cold cream to her face to remove her makeup.

"Of course. But that pretty much includes everyone at the party, except perhaps Rob and me, you and Louisa. There must have been other couples where only one knew him. But think of it: a dark house, lots of rooms and then that silly game of sardines where everyone is racing around who knows where. With masks on!"

"Yes, with masks on. But the costume identified the person," Amanda said. "We didn't know who was who until we all took off our masks." She turned around to face him as he buttoned up his pajama shirt. "What if there was someone else in the house hiding all along? Or someone in a duplicate costume?"

"Do you imagine Randy ran upstairs and changed into a Peter Pan costume, only to come back down the back stairs, propel Spencer down the basement stairs, and then go back upstairs and change into his regular evening clothes?"

"Well, not Randy. Obviously," Amanda said, turning back to the mirror to tissue off the cold cream. "He was serving drinks all night."

"There could have been someone we don't know about who was hidden in the house. That person—whoever he or she is—wouldn't have had to have a costume. The trip mechanism could have been set up at any time prior to the event. The person could have come down the back stairs or in from the backyard, done the deed and slipped back out. Remember, only the front of the house was illuminated. And with the staff working in the kitchen with the lights on, the perpetrator could clearly see when the kitchen was empty."

Amanda put the tissues in the wicker trash bin and turned again. "But why was Spencer alone on the basement stairs?"

"That is the question," Brendan said. "What do you know of him?"

"Not too much. He was always full of energy and big ideas, boisterous, you might even say loud. He and Bitsy were the odd couple. You know, the little woman who could tame the beast."

Amanda got up and turned off the dainty vanity light.

The doorbell rang. They both slumped their shoulders at the thought that sleep was still far away.

"Oh, who could it be?" Amanda asked.

Brendan put on his robe and slid his feet into slippers and went down the short hall to the top of the stairs where he could see the outline of somebody behind the frosted glass of the front door.

The bell rang again.

"Who is it?" he asked before opening the door.

"It's me, Shirley."

By this time Amanda had also put on a robe and was halfway down the stairs. "Oh, please don't let it be some plumbing problem at this hour on a weekend."

"You wanted to be a landlord," Brendan said and opened the door.

"I'm sorry. Did I wake you?" Shirley asked.

"Just about. What's the matter?"

"I need to talk to you."

"Is there a problem next door?" Brendan asked, referring to the big house.

"Not exactly." She twisted her hands together and shivered a bit.

"Come in, then."

"Thank you," she said, pulling her overcoat more tightly around her Cleopatra costume. "I didn't think it could wait." Without being invited to do so, she sat down on the sofa and pulled a packet of cigarettes and a lighter from her pocket. Observing this, Amanda went into the adjacent dining room, found the only, little-used ashtray, brought it back and handed it to the young woman.

Brendan and Amanda both sat down in the armchairs facing her and waited.

"I know who did this," Shirley said, drawing on the cigarette and exhaling.

They said nothing.

"It was Bitsy."

"What?" Amanda said, almost scoffing.

Brendan put his hand up. "What makes you say that?"

"It's obvious, isn't it?"

"I'm afraid it isn't to me. Did you see or hear something?"

"It's more like she did. Earlier in the evening while the dancing was going on, Spencer took me by the arm and pulled me into the hallway that leads to the library or study. He said he wanted to talk to me." She took another drag of her cigarette. "We'd been having a bit of a fling, you see."

Amanda's eyes opened wide.

"I wanted to end it, and even being at the party with Spencer's partner, Howard Hammond, was uncomfortable for me. I realized that we had no future together and we had a bit of an argument. He wanted to keep going on and I said I couldn't. Or wouldn't. I started to go back to the sitting room and he grabbed me by the arm. Look." She rolled up her sleeve to demonstrate slight bruising on her forearm. "I pulled away and almost ran into Bitsy, who had been standing there in the dark. I ran back into the main party."

"Did you hear them talking then or arguing?"

"I went so fast, I heard nothing. But you see? She's a jealous woman to begin with and I think she suspected something was going on with Spencer. She just didn't know it was me. She had plenty of time to set up a one-on-one meeting with Spencer for later in the evening to hash things out. Then, when she got him alone in the kitchen, she lured him to the basement and pushed him down."

Brendan's dark eyebrows went up in surprise. "That's an

interesting theory. How could she push him down the stairs when she was upstairs hiding out as a sardine?"

Shirley stammered as she searched for an explanation. "She had been to the house before many times while preparing for the party. She knew the layout of the rooms and the presence of the back stairs. My theory is that she arranged to meet Spencer while the game was going on, slipped down the back stairs, killed him and, as cool as a cucumber, sneaked back upstairs and found a hiding place. And once we joined her in her hiding place, her alibi was established. Clever, no?"

She looked from Brendan to Amanda for confirmation of her theory.

"How do you know there are back stairs that end in the kitchen?"

"Well, it's a big old house. The back stairs always go to the kitchen, don't they? Besides, Spencer gave me a tour of the house right after he got the listing. I saw it when it was all full of furniture."

Brendan stood. "Thank you for your comments. We'll take them into consideration."

Shirley stubbed her cigarette out and stood. "Here's the thing. Because she overhead Spencer and me talking—and because she has a nasty temper—I'm frightened that she'll come after me next," she said.

"It's a good thing that there's a sturdy lock on your front door. I would suggest that you make sure both front and back doors are locked at all times. If you're afraid, you risked a lot coming over here in the dark at this hour. I'll walk you back now." He pulled an overcoat from the coat rack and turned to Amanda as he put it on, making an exasperated face. "Back in a jiffy," he said.

Amanda was still in the sitting room when he came back a few minutes later. "That was pretty strange in more ways than one," he said, taking off his coat. "What's all this business about Bitsy being a jealous wife? And having a nasty temper?"

"I don't know her well enough to know if that's true, but we can always ask Louisa. Bitsy seemed pretty shocked to me."

"We'll leave all this for tomorrow. Let's get to bed."

Chapter 10

It was Sunday, but Brendan felt he had to go into the station and get the ball rolling on this new case. First, he checked in with Clyde—who was there before him, as usual.

"Has the Doc got to him yet?" he asked.

"It's early, it's the weekend and you know how he is about being pressured," Clyde replied.

"Did you get a better look at the body?"

"Actually, I did. Poor guy to leave this life dressed like that."

"Well, it was a costume party after all."

"His outfit was a bit torn up in the fall and he had a piece of black fringe in his hand."

Brendan stared. "I wonder if that was from his costume or someone else's? Amanda told me that almost everyone had that ornamentation."

"Even George Washington?"

Brendan shrugged his shoulders. "Who knows? But let me tell you about our strange encounter last night with our new tenant, Shirley, who was at the party, too."

After he finished, Clyde shook his head. "That is really an odd coincidence, don't you think? That she lives next door and was also at the party? Besides, it sounds like a tall tale to me. You were supposed to believe that the wife overheard a conversation and then just happened to have two eye screws and wire in her handbag in order to set up the trap on the steps? That's ridiculous."

"Exactly. The main rooms downstairs were fully occupied with dancers and people drinking. The likelihood that anyone could slip away to set that up on short notice doesn't fly. Bitsy, the wife, was very visible during the evening as she orchestrated the games. The only time she wasn't was when she went to hide for the sardines game. It's very clever, though. She gets back at her former lover and implicates the wife out of sheer spite, probably. Spencer's not around to deny the conversation and if Bitsy said it never happened, Shirley will maintain she's lying. "Wait a minute. If Shirley was the one who broke it off, as she told us, why would she put suspicion on Bitsy?"

"It seems more premeditated than anything. I suppose you'll need to know who had access to the house before the party. But it will all rest on finding out more about the victim and what motive someone may have had," Clyde said.

"I'm going to work on the roster for interviews that we need to get on first thing tomorrow. I may need you to help out."

"Sure thing," Clyde, who liked to keep involved in every investigation, said.

Brendan went to his office and took the guest list out of his pocket and smoothed it out on top of his desk. He sighed. Fifteen couples, some kitchen staff, the musicians and Spencer's assistants. A lot of people to interview and he wanted to get as many done as possible early on before memories dimmed and stories changed.

He decided he would have the couples done at the same time to suit his detectives' availability. These were people used to being accommodated, but they were going to have to come down to the station. He looked at the work roster for the coming week and began the task of assigning guests to his men, keeping in mind the personalities of the detectives. A few were old hands and their world-weary approach might not be the best one. Or it could be a secret weapon.

Two hours later, he finished and went home to have time to read the newspaper before he and Amanda headed out to his parents' home for Sunday dinner. He called out as he came into the house and she answered from the bedroom.

"Just getting dressed. I slept in," she said, coming to the head of the stairs and fastening an earring on.

"You look as refreshed as I wish I felt," he said, mounting the stairs.

"Have a hot bath. That might revive you," she said.

"Excellent idea. While the tub is filling up, you can fill me in on the Bitsy and Spencer relationship."

"I don't know what to tell you. She's Louisa's friend, after all. What I know is that they seemed to have a successful marriage and he has a thriving business. I don't know if I believe a word that Shirley said last night. And it makes me even more uneasy, thinking that she's one of our tenants."

"Why? Do you think she's going to throw you down the stairs?"

"That's not funny. It's just that, if it's true that they had an affair, it doesn't speak well for her morals."

"Or his," Brendan added, as he turned on the taps.

"Of course. But he's not living next door. If it isn't true, then she's a liar, which is also not a comforting thought. And the whole incident she told us about could have been made up. Oh, I don't want to think about her anymore." Amanda left him to his bath.

"THAT WAS A GREAT IDEA. Something about soaking relaxes the mind," Brendan said as they got in the car.

"Let your brain cells have a rest for now since they work overtime for most of the week. And we don't want to bore your parents with our work problems."

Brendan was one of five children and used to a boisterous household. Although neither he nor his brother, Patrick, a priest, lived at home, their space had been replaced by Bridie's husband Frank and their child Imogen. As they came up the front walk, they could hear the younger brother, Sean, playing the piano and the chatter of sisters Angela and Bridie in the living room as they entertained the baby.

Mr. Halloran heard the door open and greeted them. "How are you both? How was the party?"

"Eventful," Brendan said.

"Come in. Chaos rules, as usual."

"Hello," Bridie said from the couch, trying to contain the squirming Imogen.

Angela ran up to her much older brother and hugged him and then Amanda in turn. "You get to do all the fun things."

"Like what?" Amanda asked.

"Costume parties and stuff."

"Well, Halloween is this week," Amanda said. "We just celebrated early. Will you go trick-or-treating? What's your costume going to be?"

"I'm not sure yet. I might be a hula dancer."

"That could be a chilly decision. Do you have a grass skirt already?" Brendan asked as he passed the bottle of whiskey that he brought to his father.

"I know. I think I'll just make a lei out of paper to wear. I'll have a coat on anyway so no one will see I don't have a full costume."

"And what about Sean?"

"He said he wants to be a hobo."

"Interesting choice," Brendan said, raising his eyebrows and looking at Amanda since everyone had dismissed that costume for the Whitings' party as being too common and lacking class.

"It's easy. He just needs some of Dad's old clothes and dirt on his face," Angela said.

"Won't the clothes be too big?" Amanda asked.

"Of course. That's how hobos dress," Angela said, shaking her head at the ignorance of the question.

The piano playing stopped and Sean came in and gave his brother a hug.

"Have you grown two inches since last week?" Brendan asked.

Sean stood up even straighter at the comment.

"He's on tiptoes," Angela said pointing.

"Don't worry. I'll get there soon enough. And I'm sure I'll be taller than you, anyway."

Angela stalked over to the couch to her sister and the baby and decided to ignore her brother for the rest of the day.

"Chaos and drama," Brendan whispered to Amanda. "Let's see what my mother is up to."

Amanda followed him into the kitchen, where, from Amanda's experience, she mostly seemed to be. That day, her back was to them as she worked at the large table. Brendan put his arms around his mother, startling her before receiving a kiss.

"There you are," she said. "I'm just putting the finishing touches on the chicken. She was arranging the two hens that had come out of the oven on a serving platter. "We're ready to eat, everyone," she said in a loud voice.

Her husband hefted the platter, Brendan picked up a huge bowl of mashed potatoes, Amanda carried in the carrots that had been topped with melted butter and honey, Angela took in the rolls, Mrs. Halloran, the gravy and there was the noise of chairs being scraped back as the family sat down.

"Where's Frank?" Mr. Halloran asked.

"Here. I'm here," he said, hurrying to his seat on the other side of the baby's high chair from his wife, Bridie. "Hello, Bren and Amanda," he said.

"Let's have grace," Mr. Halloran said and everyone crossed themselves, bowed their heads while he gave a short prayer, then made the sign of the cross.

It was at moments like these that Amanda felt most awkward, because her family went to the Episcopalian church on Sunday mornings for services but religion was not a part of daily life, much less every meal.

Mr. Halloran stood and began to carve the chicken while the other dishes were passed around the table. The baby banged a spoon on the wooden high chair's tabletop.

"I see we're to have an accompaniment to the meal," Brendan said.

"She loves banging on things," Frank said.

Amid the noise and the chatter Amanda noticed that Mrs. Halloran was very quiet. She looked over at Brendan to see if he noticed but he was busy passing the rolls. Her attention went to Bridie, who had noticed the same thing.

"Is everything all right, Mama?"

"I was just thinking of your Uncle Mike. He loved making a racket as a little boy. Tomorrow would have been his birthday."

Everyone was quiet. Sean bowed his head for a moment before the motion of passing food and conversation began again. Amanda had her head down slightly but looked around at each family member. Who was Uncle Mike? Obviously, she was not going to voice her question at that moment, but it was strange that this family, which was so more open in many ways than hers was, had not given her any background. She had noticed a photograph of a young man on the piano in the other room but always assumed it was one of the Halloran boys.

"Frank, are you still enjoying working for Rob at the Oasis Club?"

"Yes, I am. And even though I studied accounting, we never got into the nuts and bolts of operating a business like his. The inventory, for example, is different for alcohol than for food, which is perishable. And if one of the bartenders decides to be more generous in mixing a drink, it can really affect the bottom line, as Rob calls it. But the food is more of a problem. What can't be sold while it's still fresh becomes lunch for the staff."

"I'm guessing that you all eat well, then," Amanda said.

"The chef is amazing. I think I'm gaining weight."

"I heard that you were looking for a chef for your tenants, is that right?" Bridie said.

"I know this is going to sound odd to you all, but these girls grew up in households where their mothers might not have done the cooking and consequently, they didn't learn. And then there are families where the mother likes to preside in the kitchen and the girls are excluded."

That got a laugh from Bridie. "The kitchen is Mama's domain unless she's in a cranky mood and then calls out asking why nobody is helping her."

"Cranky?" her mother asked. "You have no idea what it is to put together three meals a day for this tribe."

"I was only teasing, Mama. But you do need to ask for help more. Otherwise, I'll be like those girls at Brendan and Amanda's who don't know how to do anything."

"Another concern I had was that they might inadvertently set the house on fire in their attempts, so I suggested that I would provide the evening meal," Amanda said. "It has two advantages. I can keep a closer eye on how they're keeping up the place—you know, girls on their own can be quite untidy. And the other advantage is that we'll join them and I won't have to cook."

Mrs. Halloran and Bridie stared at her.

"Being like one of those girls, I never learned how," Amanda said. "I could never put together a meal like this as you do."

"I could teach you," her mother-in-law said.

"I appreciate the offer, but with working all day, I don't know that I could find the time."

Mrs. Halloran nodded with a smile but clearly felt rebuffed. "There's always the Sunday dinner," she added.

Oh, no. Stepped in it again, Amanda thought.

"That's a good idea. I could assist you and learn in the process."

"That's a good idea. I could always use an extra pair of hands."

"And you'll get to see more of Brendan," Amanda said.

Crisis resolved.

The conversation took up its usual rhythm as they made their way through the vast meal with apple pie for dessert.

"Oof," Brendan said. "I may need to take a nap when I get home."

"And you should. You work too hard," his mother said.

"After our long night, he went into the station this morning."

"Be careful, son. You don't want them taking advantage of you," Mr. Halloran said.

They said goodbye with their arms full of leftovers from the meal, a good thing since the chef she planned on hiring wouldn't work on weekends. As they got in the car, Amanda couldn't help but ask the inevitable.

"Who was Uncle Mike?" she asked.

"He was my mother's brother. Younger brother. What everyone used to call the baby of the family. Which is funny because he was a big bruiser of a man."

"Is that his photograph on the piano?"

"Yes. He was one of those people who could play by ear. Never had a lesson but could pound out a tune."

Amanda waited for more elaboration but Brendan kept his eyes on the road.

"When did he die?"

"About 15 years ago."

They drove in silence but Amanda couldn't help but ask, "How did he die?"

"He was shot."

Silence again.

"He was a policeman."

"Is that why you chose that profession?"

"Perhaps. Other things, too."

"I would imagine that was upsetting to your parents."

"Oh, yes."

"I wish you had told me this earlier. You make your work sound cerebral but there is real danger in what you do each day," Amanda said.

"Not really," he replied.

"All right. Let's be more precise. There is real danger every day. You're interviewing people who don't want to talk to you, going to parts of the city that are hardly safe, you got locked in a shed with me when we hardly knew one another and you routinely chase down bad guys."

"Sure, it's possible. But I'm not a beat cop anymore assigned to a rough neighborhood like my uncle. They never solved who did it, by the way."

They stopped at a red light. Brendan turned to her. "Don't worry, nothing is going to happen to me."

Chapter 11

Brendan had sorted through the list of guests and staff at the party. What he didn't know was the connection to Spencer and Bitsy. The only person who could reliably tell him was Louisa, who agreed to come to the station and go through it with him.

The desk sergeant was surprised to see a well-dressed young blonde woman come in from the street and ask for Lieutenant Halloran.

"He's my brother-in-law," she said before he jumped to another conclusion.

"Herb, can you take her to the boss' office?"

"Sure thing. Right this way," he looked back at the desk sergeant with a smirk.

"What brings you in today?" he said as they walked through into the restricted area.

"A murder," Louisa said.

Nothing more was said as he walked ahead of her and then stopped at Brendan's open door and knocked. "Someone here to see you."

"Thank you, Herb. Thank you, Louisa, for coming so promptly."

"My pleasure."

"You'll have to forgive Herb's gawking at you," he said after the detective had left. "Aside from Amanda, they don't usually see women like you."

"Like what?"

"Well dressed, sophisticated and self-confident."

Louisa laughed.

"Please sit down."

"This is a very nice office you've got," she said, looking around.

Brendan could tell her designer's eye was taking in every detail and she might come up with some suggestions for improvement. No black fringe, though.

"I thought that the investigation after Fred and Valerie's wedding was going to be daunting with so many guests, but you remember they were all in full view. Here we have a bunch of folks in costumes—nobody but you and maybe Bitsy knowing who was who—scattered around a dimly lit mansion and some of them racing through the upstairs room looking for the original sardine."

"I can't help you with where people were once that game began. That will be up to them. I was with Amanda since you men decided to sit it out. We were prowling around the second floor but thought that was too obvious a hiding place and went up one more story to the servants' quarters."

"What was that like?"

"Like most such accommodations for staff. Small, bare rooms that hadn't been cleaned for the party, of course. And, of course, the radiators had all been turned off. There was no way that Bitsy would have chosen the third floor for a hiding place. Much less the attic on the next floor up. We didn't even try there."

"No, you're right."

"I can tell you who the guests were according to their costumes. Keep in mind that in some cases, I only know first names."

Brendan turned the list she had given him earlier around to face her.

"I think we can eliminate some people as suspects," she said and he raised his eyebrows.

"I hope I'm not stepping on your toes, but it's obvious that it couldn't have been Rob or me. Or you and Amanda."

"Rob was drinking with me in the dining room," Brendan said.

"Randy, the barman, was at his post the entire time as far as I could see and the other assistant—maybe you took down his name?"

"Reggie."

"Yes, he was helping out, getting ice from the kitchen and attending to the guests."

"And the kitchen gals seemed to be in sight of one another the whole time," Brendan said. "There were a few more folks who came and went from the dining room, but I wasn't really paying attention to who they were."

"So, at least ten people who have alibis, not to mention no motive to shove the poor man down the stairs."

"Poor man? Amanda told me you didn't think very highly of Spencer."

"Poor man because he's dead, that's all. I think he was awfully full of himself and overbearing, at least with his staff."

"Did Bitsy ever confide in you about their relationship?" Brendan asked.

"No. And I didn't ask. She seemed unfazed when he was boisterous, although her parents weren't too enthusiastic about them getting married. They lived in a grand style, so I believe she was happy enough."

She ran her finger down the list. "Bitsy's brother was the Cop and his wife the Robber. Bruce and Anne."

"Did they get along with Spencer?"

"I really don't know. They were invited to the party, so I assumed so."

She returned to the list. "I'd say Fred and Valerie, Napoleon and Josephine, could probably be eliminated since they didn't know Spencer."

"Why were they invited?" Brendan asked.

"Frankly, they were scrambling for guests. I suggested them as well as Caroline and José, since they have the appearance of wealth, and it was supposed to be a sales presentation of sorts. By extension, Fred and Valerie. With his crushing work schedule at the hospital, he doesn't spend much time in social activities. I thought it would be fun for Valerie to get out more." She puzzled over some of the guests' names. "They all came to the salon to get fitted, but I wasn't there for some of them. I think they must have been Spencer's friends. You know, of course, that Caesar was Howard, Spencer's partner. I don't know who his Cleopatra was."

"I do. She is one of our new tenants."

"Interesting. How is that going, by the way?"

"We've only just started so I couldn't say. Amanda has managed to get someone in to cook for us all tonight."

"How cozy. Housemother and housefather," she said with a laugh.

"We'll see how that works out. Amanda was more afraid that, left to their own devices, they would burn the house down."

Louisa looked back at the list. "Julia and George, Red Riding Hood and the Wolf, were hiding upstairs with us."

"Spencer might have been dead already by then, for all we know."

"That's a chilling thought. With everyone dashing around, I can't see how you're going to figure this out. I've done all I can for now, but if something else comes to me, I'll let you know.

Off to work now," she waved.

"I'll walk you out," he said. The telephone rang.

"Go ahead and get that. I'll find my way out. I may take out my handkerchief and dab my eyes to let the fellows out there think you gave me the third degree." She giggled.

Brendan shook his head and picked up the receiver. It was the Medical Examiner.

"Broken ankle and neck. Enough alcohol in his stomach and system to have dulled the pain, however. Except he was already dead by then."

"Thanks."

"Was he a performer or in a Wild West show?"

"No. Remember, it was a Halloween costume party," Brendan said.

"For adults?" He gave a snort at the silly notion and hung up.

Brendan went out to the bullpen, an open area where the other detectives had their desks, and motioned for Dominic to come with him back to his office.

"Did you get to rest up yesterday?" Brendan asked, noticing the dark circles under the man's eyes.

"Noisy neighbors. I might have to move."

"That's the worst. You could've taken over my old place but my sister Bridie and my brother-in-law have dibs on it."

"That was fast."

"The two of them sharing a room with the baby was a tight squeeze. They'll have a place of their own. I just hope Bridie won't be lonely by herself during the day."

"She'll be back at your parents' place every day, I'm sure. Free babysitting."

"And keeping my mother company. She says things are too quiet during the week. Say, I'm about to go interview the widow, who is currently at her brother's house. Why don't you come along and see what you make of the situation?"

THEY DROVE to Brookline to a sizable Victorian house that Brendan couldn't imagine the high-flying Spencer would have been comfortable in. Interviewing the recently surviving spouse was the most important thing to do first and the meeting he always most dreaded. It was vital to get an early impression of her after the event although he had formed an opinion of her during the party as a quietly authoritative person despite her nickname.

The brother answered the door. They introduced themselves and he provided his name.

"If you don't mind, my sister has asked me to sit in on the conversation."

"Not at all. You were at the party, too, I remember," Brendan said.

"It's a good thing I was. What a horrible thing," he said in a hushed voice. They soon realized that the foyer where they stood opened to a sitting room and Bitsy was already there, sitting on the edge of her chair waiting for them.

"I'm so sorry for your loss, Mrs. Whiting," Brendan said, removing his hat. "I'm Lieutenant Brendan Halloran."

"Thank you," she said in a controlled voice. "Yes, I remember you. You're married to Amanda, aren't you?"

He nodded his head.

"This is Sergeant Dominic Barone, who will be assisting me." Dominic, who had already taken off his hat, shook her hand. "We've got most of the investigative force assigned to this."

"Terrible tragedy," Bruce said, sitting in a chair next to his sister and motioning that the detectives could occupy the couch.

"Was there anything on your husband's mind at the party?" Brendan asked.

"What do you mean?"

"Had anything unpleasant happened that day? Was he worried about anything?"

"What's that got to do with anything?" she asked.

"To get right down to it, do you have any idea why he went down to the basement after telling everyone explicitly not to go down there?"

"No idea at all. I had been down there and there's nothing to see. Perhaps that's what he meant."

"Instead of warning everyone off, he could have just locked the door to the basement," Dominic said.

She glared at him. "I don't know why he said that. And I certainly don't know why he went down there."

"Did you take a tour of the house with him prior to the party?"

"Several times, but I knew the layout of the house well. I used to play with the Williams' son when I was little. We loved playing hide-and-seek because there were so many rooms."

Brendan looked up from writing in his small notebook. "I was under the impression that the late Mr. Williams had no family. Somebody told me that the proceeds of the sale had been earmarked for some charity."

"That's correct," Bitsy said. "His son was estranged from his father for quite some time."

"Was everything all right with your husband? Health? Finances?"

"Of course. You saw him. A man in the prime of his life. Business doing well."

"Happy home life," Bruce added.

"That's good to know," Brendan said. "Do you know why he asked the staff to leave the kitchen at one point?"

"How should I know? I was carrying the entire load of the party's entertainment. And by that time, I was busy trying to find the best hiding place. Have you asked them?"

"I didn't get a definitive answer, and I will be interviewing them again to get more details." Brendan looked down at his notebook. "There's nothing going on that you know of that would be a threat to your husband's life?"

"Absolutely nothing. He was successful and well-liked. He was a good provider and now I don't know what I'm going to do." She broke down in tears at that point and her brother shot the detectives a nasty look.

"Do you have anything to add, sir?" Brendan asked.

"Yes. They had a happy marriage and solid support from the family, too. This is a travesty and I hope you find out what happened."

"Where were you when Mr. Whiting was discovered?"

"I was upstairs engaged in a half-hearted attempt to join in the frivolity. I was more interested in looking at Mr. Williams' library than getting squashed in a closet. I don't think he was a collector of first editions as such, but he had a marvelous bookshelf full of travel journals. I can't imagine anything more exciting than taking off for the Middle East and wandering around for months at a time."

"Except I won't let him," a woman said as she came into the room.

"This is my wife, Anne," Bruce said. "As if you couldn't guess."

"I remember you both from the other night. The old-fashioned police office and the robber. Clever costumes," Brendan said, remembering how the husband was outfitted more like a London bobby of the last century and his wife looked like a scruffy newsboy with a snap brim cap, accessorized by a bag presumably of loot.

"Have you got any leads yet?" she asked.

"We've just begun talking to people," Brendan said.

"I'd look closely at the musicians. They seemed a little shady to me." She stood behind her husband's chair."

"In what way?"

"A little too slick, and certainly a little too familiar with some of the female guests."

Bitsy turned to look at her sister-in-law. "I didn't notice anything of the kind. They came highly recommended."

Anne shrugged her shoulders. "You were rather busy as mistress of ceremonies and probably didn't notice. By the way, why did you have that role and not Spencer?"

"He wanted to mingle with the guests and get a sale if possible. The executor was willing to give him a bonus if the house sold within the first month of listing."

"That's interesting. When everyone took off their masks, I didn't recognize many people for one thing. And many seemed too young to afford such a place. Who put together the guest list?"

"If you'd like to talk about party planning, let's discuss it at some other time," Mrs. Whiting said sharply. Her sister-in-law blinked dramatically and left the room.

"As you can tell, emotions are still raw. If you need to contact my sister again, please call me first." Bruce stood up.

"Sir, I can't promise that I won't have to contact her again. There may be some details that come up that need clarification. If you feel you need to be present during such a conversation, we'll be happy to accommodate you."

Brendan and Dominic didn't speak until they were in the car and on their way back to the station.

"You could have cut the air with a knife between those two women," Dominic said.

"Her brother may want to be her protector, but I bet she'll be back in her own home soon enough."

Chapter 12

Brendan got back home to find Amanda pacing the living room floor.

"Where've you been?" she asked.

"Work, of course. What's the matter?" he said, taking off his coat.

"First, you might want to put that back on. We're due at the big house for the first meal prepared by the cook."

"Now?"

"Yes, now."

"Do I get to sit down and peruse the evening paper first?"

"Absolutely not."

"Or pour myself a tot of sherry?"

"Again, no. I had to beg, borrow and steal to get this woman—any woman, actually—and we don't want to sashay in late to a cold meal and the glare of my new hire."

"It never ceases to amaze me how you folks are so intimidated by your cooks."

"What do you mean, 'you people'?"

"Where did you find this gem?"

"Our cook recommended her, of course."

"Ah, that explains everything. It's not just your reputation on the line but Cook's as well. You know, I don't even know her real name," Brendan said.

"That's not important now. If you need to wash up, fine. Otherwise, we can just go over now." Amanda looked at her wristwatch. "It's important that we be on time. We don't want to set a bad example."

Brendan sighed. "Will there be beer or wine at dinner?"

"Of course not," she said, tugging on his reluctant sleeve and starting to drag him out the door.

"Let me wash my hands and comb my hair at least," he complained, going upstairs quickly. "I'm ready," he said, coming down the stairs.

As he locked the front door behind them, he asked, "What is this big wooden bench doing here anyway?" pointing to the large object with its peeling paint adjacent to the entrance.

"I don't know. Obviously, it came with the house. We could repaint it, you know. It's very handy to set down packages while I'm fishing for the keys in my handbag."

"That's its only purpose?"

"We could have pots of geraniums there in the summer," she suggested. "Wouldn't that be cheery?"

They arrived at the big house, as they were now used to calling it, through the back door, which was certainly more informal but quicker than traipsing through the yard around to the front. It also gave Amanda the opportunity to introduce Brendan to the new cook.

They wiped their feet carefully on the back doormat and went through the mud room, where they hung up their coats, into the steamy and fragrant kitchen.

"Hello!" Amanda called out.

The woman at the stove turned around and shouted, "Young Brendan, if my eyes don't deceive me!"

"Mrs. O'Reilly!" he responded with equal surprise. She dashed toward him and got him in a bear hug before releasing him quickly.

"Don't want to scorch the gravy," she said, going quickly back to the stove. Over her shoulder she said, "Go out to your girls. We'll catch up after the meal."

"Very clever," Brendan said to Amanda. "A spy in the kitchen."

"Of course."

"Remind me who is who."

"You met Shirley at the Whitings' party. Then there's Gretchen, an old friend of hers, I gather, and they look remarkably alike. Not their features, but hair color and build. You know how it is with best friends copying each other's look. Then there's Rebecca, with the red hair, and Dassie."

"Who?'

"That's what everyone calls her. Very polite and quiet."

"Well, introduce me around so I can cement in my brain who they are."

They went from the kitchen into the dining room. Nobody was there. They walked through to the sitting room and saw the four young women seated and talking quietly. They stood up as soon as they saw their landlords.

"Good evening, Mrs. Halloran. Mr. Halloran," they said in unison,

"I know you met them before, but this is Dassie, Rebecca, Shirley and Gretchen."

"Good evening, ladies," he said, noticing that they had been partaking of a glass of sherry before dinner and bemoaning his loss.

"I believe Cook is almost ready with the meal. Why don't we proceed to the dining room?" Amanda suggested, leading the way and seating herself at one end of the table. She nodded for Brendan to occupy the opposite end, with the girls taking up the other four seats.

"How has everything been?" Amanda asked.

"Just fine. What a lovely house," Rebecca said. "My parents were thrilled we're in a nice neighborhood and get our weekday meals as well."

"That's good to hear," Amanda said. "So many times young women on their own have to settle for whatever they can find and it's not always so pleasant. Peanut butter on crackers for dinner."

"Were you once a renter?" Rebecca asked.

"No. I lived with my parents until I married. I got quite used to the luxuries of living at home."

"I'd like to do that as well," Shirley said. "But my family lives in Worcester. Too far to commute, obviously."

"Is that how you know each other?" Amanda asked, looking at Gretchen who she remembered had listed a family contact with an address there.

"Yes. We went to school together. Two peas in a pod," Gretchen said.

The look on Shirley's face said that she didn't entirely agree with that assessment.

"I really wanted to enjoy life in the big city and she joined me," Shirley said.

"We work together, too," Gretchen added.

"Where's that?" Brendan asked, not having been involved in vetting the potential residents but also feigning innocence.

"At Hammond & Whiting," Shirley said. She gave him a sharp look as if to remind him of her late-night visit.

"Right."

"I'm an assistant to Howard Hammond. Gretchen is a secretary."

The swinging door from the kitchen to the dining room opened and Mrs. O'Reilly came in, bearing a platter of brisket.

"Here you go," she said, returning to her lair and coming back with boiled potatoes and gravy. One last trip brought out green beans with sliced almonds, something Brendan had never seen before.

"Now, when you're finished, there is dessert on the counter in the kitchen. I'm done for the night and you girls will take care of the clean-up, right?"

Four pairs of eyes stared at the cook.

"There we go, then. Enjoy your meal. Be sure to put any leftovers in the refrigerator and cover it carefully with wax paper," she said, bustling out.

Brendan suppressed a smile, realizing these four girls had not been expecting such a swift departure with a chore thrown at them as well.

"Sorry, I forgot to tell you all about the arrangement I made with the cook," Amanda said before they could react verbally to their new clean-up duties. "But I've got a maid coming in twice a week to do dusting, vacuuming and trash of the common rooms."

"That's a relief," Rebecca said.

"Since you all work full-time jobs, there won't be much cleaning to do. I expect you to keep your own rooms clean and in order."

A frown from Dassie suggested she thought the maid would tend to their rooms, too.

Amanda felt she had offered them something special in the rental agreement with housing and food for them and was not going to pay someone to pick up discarded stockings and clean off cluttered vanity tables. Besides, the other half of those two days the maid would be devoted to cleaning Amanda and Brendan's place. She smiled to herself at the clever way the household chores were working out.

"Pardon me," Brendan said, "but what kind of work do you do, Rebecca?"

"I'm teaching history and civics at St. Margaret's School."

"That sounds interesting."

"It doesn't pay as well as the public schools, but the girls come from good families and are very well behaved. Some of my friends from teachers college who work in the public schools have hair-raising tales about their pupils. Fights breaking out and terrible language."

"Gosh, I don't remember school being like that," Brendan said. "Then again, it was Catholic school and you had to toe the line."

"The other benefit is that, when I get married next year, they won't let me go because of it."

"Such a stupid rule," Shirley said, shaking her head.

"Also, my fiancé teaches there and as a married couple they may give us on-campus housing."

"You mean like a housemother or housemaster?" Amanda asked.

"Yes, the couple that's been doing it for a few years is retiring."

"Sounds like a nice situation," Dassie said, without much expression.

"And what do you do?" Brendan asked her.

"I work at Filene's department store. I'm on my feet most of the day, but they give us a discount on anything we buy." She tried a small smile.

"Now you tell us what you two do," Shirley said to Amanda, knowing full well.

"I work as a private investigator at my father's law firm," Amanda said.

"Oh, that sounds fascinating," Rebecca said.

"It is interesting. It's the kind of job where you learn something new every day."

"That's the best kind of job to have, to my mind. Strangely enough, while teaching, I learn something new every day, too."

"Like what?" Dassie asked.

"Aside from facts and the stories behind world events, I'm always surprised by the different way students think and express themselves. What do you do, Mr. Halloran?"

"I'm a police detective," he said.

Gretchen's eyes widened.

Shirley looked at her friend. "Sure, I told you that, didn't I? He was at the party when—"

"Don't say it!" Gretchen said.

"I don't talk about my work for entertainment purposes, don't worry," he said.

"Remind me what you do, Gretchen," Amanda said, smoothing things over.

"I work at Hammond & Whiting," she said. "Like Shirley said."

"She's in the typing pool. I got enlisted to work with the bosses," Shirley said and gave a hard look at Brendan and Amanda as if daring them to reveal how much she had blurted to them the other night.

"Shirley gets to do the fun stuff like getting that party organized," Gretchen said.

"I thought it might have been Bitsy who did that," Amanda suggested.

"It was partly her idea but she wasn't going to make sure the food got there or the invitations went out in time. I was the one who worked scheduling the guests to go to that fancy salon for costumes, too."

"My sister, Louisa, works there," Amanda said.

"Oh. I didn't realize that was your sister," Shirley said. "She has good taste."

"She's always loved fashion and she designs many of the dresses there."

"Really. Oh, I'd love to do that," Gretchen said.

Shirley gave a bit of a snort. "Don't be ridiculous. "You can't even draw!"

"I meant I would love to wear clothes like that."

Amanda tilted her head, wondering how she knew about Louisa.

"I was telling her all about the salon when we were getting ready for the party. Your sister wore one beautiful suit after another."

"Did she design all the costumes, too?" Gretchen asked.

"Silly, I told you she had. Let's not talk about the party," Shirley said.

"Let's not," Amanda said, glad to change the subject. "Well, what do you think of the meal so far?" she asked.

"Very good. Like my mother's home cooking," Rebecca said. "Nothing like the cafeteria school lunches. Chipped beef on toast—ugh! Gooey salty sauce with little meat bits on soggy bread."

"Gosh, I've never had that," Dassie said.

"Lucky you."

"My mother makes all these wonderful Swedish foods. A lot of fish dishes, too," Dassie said.

"That's good to know. I'll ask Mrs. O'Reilly if she has any special recipes. We might need that for Friday nights if any of you need to refrain from meat."

There were blank looks.

Okay, no practicing Roman Catholics here, she thought.

"And weekends you're on your own."

"I'm sure we can wrangle a meal out of our dates," Shirley said.

"I think I told you that Brendan and I won't be here on Wednesday night. It's when we dine with my parents."

"That's nice," Dassie said. "Just talking about my mother is making me a little bit homesick."

"Surely you can go home for the weekends, can't you?" Amanda asked. "I think there is a train and also the bus."

"Now you've got me thinking," Dassie said. "I bet I could leave after work on Friday and be back Sunday night. Gee, that would be swell." Her face lit up.

"Come on, let's clear these dishes and get into that apple pie," Shirley said, getting up and urging the others. "We've got a lot of work ahead of us." She glanced over at Amanda and Brendan, who remained seated. When the girls had left the dining room, Amanda suppressed a smile while Brendan raised his eyebrows at the girl's cheeky attitude.

Chapter 13

The first thing Amanda did after getting to work the next day was to make a beeline for her father's office.

"Mr. Burnside? Are you busy with something?"

He smiled back at her. "No, Miss Burnside. Please sit down."

They had long ago decided to keep up the formality at work because she especially thought it would be ridiculous to address him as 'Daddy' in such a setting. And he thought it best for her to retain her maiden name in the workplace.

"What can I help you with?"

"Did anyone here work with the late Mr. Williams?"

"No."

"Do you know anything about the disposition of his estate?"

"It's not a pretty picture but it's common knowledge. He had that huge house and a fair amount of money. In cash and gold. He and his only child, a son, were estranged for some time."

"What was that about?"

"I don't think it was anything significant. Just one of those adolescent rebellions that young men often go through and irk fathers. Sometimes, I think, only to irk their fathers."

"So, they were not reconciled when the older man died?"

"No. The interesting thing is that the father, who was a bit of a misanthrope, decided that he was fed up with the Boston attorneys and went and hired some youngster from out of town. He left everything to several charitable organizations. I can find out what they were with a phone call if you like," he said.

"No. That's not necessary." Amanda thought a moment. "Yes, actually. That might be helpful."

"Has someone hired you to look into this?"

"No. Just my insatiable curiosity. That's a harsh action to take against one's only offspring, don't you think?"

Mr. Burnside steepled his hands in front of his face. "People have done such callous things since time immemorial. There were some indications that the lawyer who drew up the will didn't know that there was a child. He was shocked when the man showed up to challenge the will and, of course, lost. Too little, too late, as they say."

"Do you know his name? Does he live in Boston?"

"The son? Why all the interest?"

"No reason. Just curious. It's a sad situation." She paused. "What do you know about Hammond & Whiting, the real estate company?"

"I haven't had any dealings with them. I gather they are—or were—the up-and-coming folks. The terms I heard used were 'hustle' and 'moxie.' They very wisely contacted all the estate attorneys in town early on in their formation, with the intent to plant in those legal minds that they were the two men who could quickly liquidate the real property of deceased clients. I understand one firm in town even gives a bonus if the land, house or commercial building sells within a certain amount of time. Don't quote me on that. It might just be business gossip."

"What is interesting is that the costume party was intended to be a way of showcasing the home in order to sell it. But Louisa told me that Spencer had a hard time inviting the sort of people who might be potential buyers. People with money. It turned out that most of the guests were young folks, and Bitsy ended up inviting friends and friends of friends just to fill out the guest list. However, they managed to get the society pages of the **Boston Globe** to send a photographer to take shots of the glamorous event. Everyone had on a mask, so for all the readers knew, it could have been the Cabots and the Lodges."

Her father chuckled. "Ingenious, actually. It seems Whiting was quite the showman."

"Until he wasn't."

Amanda was quiet a moment as she considered something. "I have become known to the big banks in town due to my financial investigations. I wonder if the Police Department would consider hiring me as a consultant to do that for this case."

"You mean Brendan."

She gave a short laugh. "It might seem more legitimate if someone else made the suggestion. Such as Detective Owens, who heads the tech unit. Do you think that seems rather forward of me? Or does it look like I'm using a personal connection for private gain?" Amanda pursed her lips with discomfort.

"My dear, the world of business, finance and almost everything else is predicated on putting oneself forward. You can't be a shrinking violet and expect to get anywhere. What's the worst that could happen when you ask?"

"They might say no?"

"Is that so bad? And if they do, give them some time and ask again in a slightly different way. Persistence pays off, you know. Sometimes people say yes just to get you off their back. Well, that's it for my nuggets of advice for the day."

"Thanks, Daddy. Er, Mr. Burnside."

Amanda felt buoyed by their chat and considered that her parents may have had their reservations about some of her choices, but they never outright discouraged her. Thinking about the late Mr. Williams and his broken relationship with his son, she felt quite lucky to have such supportive parents. She sat at her desk, picked up the phone, called the main number at the police station and asked to speak to Detective Clyde Owens.

AT THE SAME TIME, Brendan and Dominic were on their way to the offices of Hammond & Whiting in the financial district, having called ahead to let the remaining lead partner know of their arrival. It was their intention to talk to Mr. Hammond, Randy and the other assistant who had acted as doorman at the party. Brendan also wanted to talk to Shirley out of the context of their roles as landlord and tenant; he felt it important to keep his personal and professional lives as separate as possible.

The real estate company occupied two floors of one of the trendiest buildings and had outfitted it as the lair of energetic and prosperous young businessmen. Potted plants adorned the reception area and a workman in overalls was busy testing the dryness of the soil of each plant and watering accordingly as they came in. The receptionist sat behind a gleaming desk that had a telephone, a notepad and a single red rose in a vase. The flower matched her lipstick and nail polish perfectly.

"Good morning, gentlemen. How may I help you?" She might have just stepped out of a beauty parlor with her perfectly waved hair that fell in soft curls above the shoulders of her powder blue suit.

Brendan handed over his card and explained that he had contacted Hammond earlier. In the background, they could hear telephones ringing that must have been connected through a switchboard. The telephone she picked up functioned more like an intercom and she spoke a few phrases softly.

"Randy will be out in a moment to assist you. Please make yourselves comfortable."

They sat on chairs a fair distance from her desk, presumably not to inadvertently overhear her whispered announcements.

"Who's Randy?" Dominic asked.

"He's the dogsbody that was enlisted to be the bartender at the party. He was one of the few not in costume."

"Is being a bartender part of his job description, do you think?"

"Jack-of-all-trades kind of thing, I suppose."

Randy had them wait ten minutes while they stared at the wood-paneled walls and the receptionist, who sat with hands folded on the desk until her direct line rang and she spoke quietly then hung up.

Dominic put his head down so only Brendan could hear him. "Is that what she does all day? How much do you think she gets paid?"

"Why, are you thinking of ditching the department?"

"Are you kidding? I couldn't afford the wardrobe for one thing. And I'd be bored stiff just sitting there all day."

"Just ornamental to impress the likes of peasants like us."

Randy finally came out of a door at the other end of the reception area and gave them a sad smile.

"I'm sorry to have kept you waiting. So much to do," he said, suggesting that he was helming the aftermath of Spencer's demise. "I've got a small conference room that we can use."

"We'd like to talk to Mr. Hammond."

"Certainly. That would be in his office. But I understood that you wanted to talk to me as well."

"Yes, and the other assistant from your office who was at the party."

"Reggie. Yes, he knows. This way, please," he said.

Dominic wondered if Randy was an aspiring theater actor by his slim-fitted suit and affected way of speaking and talking. He was happy to know that his comfortable clothes sufficed for his job, but most of all that he was not someone's assistant, whatever that meant. Once again, his brain was turning over the thought of how much money the job paid, as he often pondered money matters. Not that he would ever consider such a job.

"Here we are," Randy said, opening the door to a small room that had a table and two chairs on each side, likely a place where contracts could be signed.

The two detectives sat down and took off their coats and hats.

"Can you tell me how long you've worked here?" Brendan began.

"Three years now. I began in the mailroom and then there was an opening for an assistant to Mr. Whiting."

"Was there someone in that position before you."

Randy hesitated a moment, clearly not expecting that question. "Why, yes. He moved on."

"On good terms?"

"I really don't know."

"Oh, come on, Randy. In an office like this everyone knows the gossip. What did you hear?"

Randy's face flushed a bit and, being aware of the giveaway, he spoke up. "I gathered that Mr. Whiting was not in favor of his performance. When I was hired, I was told what I was to do along with a long list of what *not* to do."

"That's interesting. What were some of the 'nots'?"

Randy adjusted the left shirtsleeve cuff carefully. "Not to talk about the company's business outside of the office. One could assume that the former assistant may have leaked information to a competitor."

"One could. It sounds like real estate can be a cutthroat business."

"It's very competitive. There is a lot of confidential information shared, dealing with proposals, bids, et cetera."

"So, you know to keep your ears open and you mouth shut," Brendan said.

"In a manner of speaking."

"Now that Mr. Whiting is deceased, what can you tell me of his relationship with his partner, Mr. Hammond."

Randy paused. "What do you want to know?"

"Were they partners or former rivals? Old friends or new allies?"

"I think there was a healthy competition to see who could garner the agents with the most listings and highest sales figures. But it was all in good-humored fun."

"Now to the party. I know you were behind the bar for the entire evening. Did you hear or see anything strange?"

"I was too busy dealing with the drinks to pay attention to what the guests were doing, to be quite honest."

"Had you been to the house before?"

"Yes. Several times. Mr. Whiting hired some men to move the furniture from the ground-floor rooms upstairs, thank goodness. But Reggie, Shirley and I were tasked with making sure there were enough chairs, dinnerware and glasses for the guests. The former owner had all of that. It was just a matter of finding it. Also locating the restrooms and making sure they were suitable for the guests. Two of Mr. Whiting's household staff came over, too, to make sure that things were clean and the floors swept in preparation."

"That's quite a lot of work."

"Yes. But that's the job. I did what the boss wanted."

"Now that the boss is no longer here, what happens to you?"

"Mr. Hammond confirmed that my job is secure," Randy said with his small smile.

"Had you been down to the basement while you were preparing the house?"

"No, I had no reason to. All my work was above ground, so to speak."

"Do you know Mrs. Whiting?"

"Of course. She was instrumental in planning the event."

"Did she and her husband get along?" Brendan asked.

"I only saw them together on a few occasions. I would say yes, they did. Why do you ask?"

"It's my job to ask intrusive questions. How did you like working for Mr. Whiting?"

"It paid well and I met interesting people."

"I mean, how did you like working for the man. It seemed like he liked to shout a lot," Brendan said, remembering Spencer's boisterous exit from the kitchen at the party.

He gave a small shrug. "Some people tend to be like that."

"Why did he ask you to be the bartender? You clearly knew what you were doing. Had you worked in that capacity before?"

Randy hesitated. "Yes, I did work as a substitute bartender for a short while some time ago." He did not elaborate where and Brendan didn't ask. Not just yet.

"Is there anything else you'd like to share with us at this time?"

"No. Just that this is a terrible thing. For me and the firm." He stood up and shook hands with both of the detectives. "I'll get Reggie."

Brendan and Dominic looked at each other.

"I get the feeling that he didn't like the old boss all that much," Dominic said.

"Spencer Whiting was a big person and personality. I can't imagine how that young man, so refined in dress and manner and careful how he speaks, tolerated his boss." Brendan said with a shrug.

"Takes all kinds. And sometimes contradictory personalities can complement each other."

There was a knock on the door and it opened to the other assistant, who had acted as doorman for the party.

"Hello," he said and introduced himself.

He looked to be younger than Randy and possibly still growing as his pants were a tad short. But he had an open face and easy manner as they took preliminary information from him about name, position and how long he had worked there.

"You were the doorman at the party, correct?" Brendan asked.

"Yes. And the person who handed out the masks to those who forgot theirs at home or were thinking they could get away without wearing one."

"Was anyone resistant?" Brendan asked, remembering that after a while he felt wearing a mask was a nuisance.

"No. In fact, most people came with theirs in place."

"What did you do when everyone had arrived?"

"I hung out at the makeshift bar with Randy, getting ice from the kitchen and collecting used glasses to bring in and get washed. Mostly I got to watch the festivities."

"You helped with the party setup, correct?"

"The physical part, yes. Not the games and all that. I helped deliver the alcohol and moved chairs around. Also, I was there early when the caterers came with the food."

"Did you go upstairs at any time before or during the party?"

"No, there were movers who took furniture upstairs so I didn't get in their way. I confined myself to the first floor."

"Did you go to the basement at any time?" Brendan asked.

"Of course not. I didn't know where the door to it was, to begin with. I only found out later when Mr. Whiting's body was found."

"Are you happy in your job?" Brendan asked.

That seemed to throw him for a loop. "Well, sure. The pay is good, the work's not too hard and it changes all the time. I'd go crazy in a job where you do the same thing all day long."

"I'm with you on that, brother," Dominic said.

Brendan glanced over at the sergeant at that unexpected remark but turned his attention once again to the assistant. "Did you see anyone besides the servers go into the kitchen?"

"No. Just myself and Randy once the party started."

"Did you notice anything unusual at all?"

"Aside from a bunch of rich people acting silly and running around in a deserted mansion, no."

Chapter 14

"Let's take a break," Brendan suggested when Reggie had left the room. They both got up and stretched from having sat so long, and Dominic tilted his head from side to side producing a satisfying cracking noise.

"We'll just talk to Shirley, the secretary, or whatever her position is, and Mr. Hammond, and then I'm going to need a very satisfying lunch."

"Agreed," Dominic said rubbing his hands together.

"Will you see if she's out there?"

Dominic looked out into the hall and saw the young woman sitting in a chair, looking very prim with her hands in her lap. He wondered if she had overhead any of the conversation with Reggie.

"This way, Miss…"

"Butler," she responded with a small smile.

"Good morning, Lieutenant Halloran," she said when she entered the room.

"This is Sergeant Barone. He'll be assisting me."

"Nice to meet you," she said.

"I understand in our discussions with the two assistants just now that you also helped set up the party scene."

"That's right."

"But you worked as Mr. Whiting's secretary?"

"Not exactly. I started out as his secretary and then became his executive assistant. I managed his calendar and appointments and any personal matter that he required. The party was of great importance to him as he hoped to get an interested buyer from the gala."

"Did you also work with Mrs. Whiting?" Brendan asked.

"Yes, she put together the guest list and I helped her send out the invitations and follow up with confirmations."

Brendan noticed how calm Shirley was. Didn't she remember that late-night confession about the affair with Spencer? Was that now just long-gone history?

"So, you were in the Williams house several times."

"Oh, yes. Mrs. Whiting wanted everything just so. She had Randy pull a low bookcase over to the corner and turn it around so that it became the bar. And the shelves behind had their books taken down and put in a far room to make space for the bottles of alcohol. It was quite ingenious."

"Did she also direct that the rooms be emptied of furniture?"

"Mr. Whiting was opposed to the idea. He said he thought the house would be more sellable—that was his favorite term—if it looked inhabited. But Mrs. Whiting, for all her diminutive size, can be quite forceful, and she said the furniture had to be moved out. It did make the place look much larger when the movers came in and did as she suggested."

"You weren't working the evening of the party as were the other assistants?"

"No. I was Mr. Hammond's date for the evening. He's been a bachelor for some time and a bit shy around women. I think he felt comfortable enough with me."

"You were the only staff person from the firm who got to attend the event as a guest?" Brendan asked.

Shirley acted as if she hadn't thought of her attendance in that way. "I suppose you're right. It was a fun evening." Her small smile disappeared. "Until tragedy struck."

"How was your relationship with Mr. Whiting recently?"

It was obvious that Shirley had not forgotten her revelations to Brendan and Amanda but she put up a good front with Dominic, who was unaware of the exact text of that late-night conversation. She directed her response to the sergeant.

"I'd worked for him for about two years and we got along well. I admired his energy and commitment to the company," she said.

"Were you in the kitchen at all that night?"

"That night? No. I had been in there with Randy or Reggie or both in the days preceding, looking at what glassware, dishes and utensils were available for use. We set them out for whatever kitchen staff would come in and wash them."

"Were you aware of the location of the basement?"

She tittered. "Under the house, I assumed."

"I meant the access to the basement."

"Of course not. We were busy in the kitchen and the pantry taking inventory. The house hadn't been inhabited for some time and it was quite dusty. I started to think that it was not the proper venue for a party, much less showing the property to its best advantage. It turned out that clearing out the dining and sitting rooms and creating atmospheric lighting made the place seem even larger than it was. Mr. Whiting was very clever with what they call staging."

"Did you see anyone go into the kitchen from the dining room during the evening?"

"I was there as the guest of Mr. Hammond. It was not my job to monitor who went where. We were involved in dancing and partaking in the games Mrs. Whiting had devised. I went off in search of her when the sardines game began. It was only then that the hue and cry went up about poor Mr. Whiting. A dreadful sound."

"So, you were upstairs with the sardines folks?"

"Yes. I was one of the first to find her."

"Bravo."

"I did cheat a bit. When we were touring the house initially, she told me that she knew the former owner's son as a child and that they played hide-and-seek in the many rooms. When we got to the room with the big dustcloths, she paused and nodded her head. I knew exactly what was going through her mind. She had let slip earlier about the games she had planned and I thought she's going to hide under those drop cloths. And she did!"

"Perhaps we ought to employ you as a detective," Dominic said.

Brendan gave him a cautionary look and took up the questioning. "What did you do when you heard all the excitement down below?"

"We trooped out very quickly and down the stairs. The yelp had come from the kitchen and, well, you were there," she added.

"Let me ask you something. Is the business healthy?"

"I should think so," she said. "Just look at this office space."

"It is impressive. Did the partners get along?"

She hesitated a moment. "Yes, they did. But they liked to have friendly little competitions with one another. In fact, all the time. Like, how much they could make someone pay for a property or what commission they got on a deal. One-upmanship, you know?"

"What happens to the business now?"

"You'll have to ask Mr. Hammond."

"I plan on doing so," Brendan said. standing up. "Would you let him know we'll meet in his office?"

Shirley seemed surprised that the interview was over. "Don't you need to ask me anything else?"

"Not just yet."

"Very well. See you at dinner," she said.

Dominic waited until she was out of earshot. "Cheeky girl. You think she's got her eye on the new boss?"

"I wouldn't put it past her."

They gathered their things and made their way to Mr. Hammond's office, a corner suite at the opposite end of the floor from Whiting's. Brendan made a mental note to have that office locked up until they could properly search it.

"Gentlemen, please come in," Mr. Hammond said, coming out from behind his enormous desk and holding out a hand. "This terrible, sad business. I don't know how we'll go on without Spencer. We met in college, you know. Please, sit down." He motioned to two wine-colored leather armchairs. He took his position back behind his desk in a chair whose back rose well above his head.

"We got the idea of starting this business together and launched it shortly after the Crash. Terrible timing! Crazy young fools that we were. Our secret? We worked harder and better than everyone else. Lots of fellows gave up on real estate while we understood that it was just the time people were trying to unload their houses to scrape together some cash. Cheaper to rent and you always have that cushion of savings. But to tell the truth, most people still stuffed it under the mattress. People were still leery of banks. And how do I know about the mattresses? Because we bought a house as a rental investment and sure enough, there was a couple of hundred dollars there!" He chuckled at the memory, then seeing his guests were not smiling, put on a serious expression. "But you're not here to listen to my stories."

"No. I wanted to ask you about your whereabouts during the sardines game. I stayed down in the dining room with some other people, yet you weren't there. Were you upstairs hunting down Bitsy?"

"I didn't dare try to climb the stairs in that clumsy Caesar costume. I was tripping over it as it was. I can't understand how ancient Romans got anything done with all that fabric flapping around their ankles."

"I believe the costume represented a Roman Senator or Consul dressed for an official assembly. Your average Roman wore a knee-length tunic," Brendan said.

"History major, am I right?" Hammond asked.

"Classics, actually," Brendan said.

"*Veni, vidi, vici,*" Hammond said and translated for Dominic's benefit. "I came, I saw, I conquered."

"I understand Italian. And it's a pretty famous phrase."

"Very good," Brendan said. "History major?" he inquired of Hammond.

"Yes, indeed. My father thought it was silly, but you can learn a lot from the past."

"Back to modern times for a moment, where were you when the sardines game began?"

"I'm a little embarrassed to say it, but I was in a bathroom. I must have eaten something dodgy for dinner earlier. I was lucky enough to find a restroom on the first floor a ways back down the hallway. I was in there longer than I'd like to admit, bogged down by all that fabric. Then I heard the yelp from the kitchen and washed up and came out to the sitting room and saw everyone congregating in the kitchen. Poor Spencer. He could barely walk in those ridiculous boots."

"He didn't trip, you know. Someone had rigged up a wire across one of the steps and he tumbled full force down to the cement cellar."

Hammond cringed. "That's awful. I didn't know that. So, you think it was deliberate?"

"How could it have been anything else?" Brendan said.

"Why did he tell everyone to stay away from the basement?" Hammond leaned forward. "Maybe Spencer set the trap for someone else. And then agreed to meet them down there, thinking they'd get there first."

"That doesn't follow. If he set up a trap, then he would have expected to find someone else's body at the base of the stairs. Not his own."

"Good point," Hammond said, rubbing his chin with his hand and looking down at his desk.

Dominic looked over at Brendan, puzzled by the man's lack of logic.

"Well, I certainly can't explain what happened or who did it," Hammond concluded.

"We didn't expect you to. That's our job. Let me switch gears for a moment. What happens to the business now?"

"It reverts to me, actually," he said as if it had just occurred to him.

"Not his wife?"

"No. He wasn't married when we put the business together. We'd heard horror stories about divorces and businesses being part of the spoils. We kept it a clean partnership between us."

"In hindsight, that was smart. But poor Mrs. Whiting gets nothing."

Hammond's face flushed a bit. "Yes, I know. But it's not as if she's destitute. Spencer had a significant real estate portfolio of his own, separate from our partnership. I'm sure she'll be fine."

"Let's hope so," Brendan said. "We don't have any more questions just yet, but it is important that his office be secured. Locked. We'll need to do a thorough search and see if there are any clues to be found there."

"Oh," Hammond said blinking. "I had asked Shirley yesterday to tidy up his office. There may be some contracts pending that I need to follow up on."

"I'm sure that can wait another few days. We need to go through his things first."

"In that case…"

"Thank you for your time, Mr. Hammond." Brendan shook the man's hand with Dominic following suit.

They didn't say a word until they got in the elevator and the doors shut.

"Do you think he's as clueless as he pretends?" Dominic asked.

"It's funny, but sometimes people can be oblivious about many things yet very good at others. He's obviously a good salesperson to have built up the business with Whiting but be glad he's not on the police force with us."

"Do you buy his alibi of being in the bathroom while Whiting met his demise?"

"We can hardly check, can we? There are too many people and too many rooms and we haven't got a motive yet."

They came out on the street and walked to the corner. The aroma of a hotdog pushcart wafted their way. They turned their heads in unison.

"Oh, that smells good," Dominic said.

"Yeah, but the vendor looks as if he hasn't washed his hands since the Great War. We don't want to spend our afternoon holed up the department's bathroom."

"Nobody would appreciate that," Dominic agreed. "There's a luncheonette down that way," he pointed. "They do a hearty pea soup with the great taste of ham hock in the broth."

"Let's do it," Brendan said and they hastened their steps.

Chapter 15

Amanda allowed herself to feel smug at the notion that Detective Owens supported her proposal to dig into the finances of Hammond & Whiting. She could tell by his enthusiasm that he would have liked to tackle it himself but didn't have the time or perhaps the expertise. The other consideration was how she was going to bill the department as Brendan's wife and landed on the idea of using her father's firm's name rather than her own. She didn't want to get Brendan into any difficulty.

She was such a familiar face in the downtown banks from her previous research that the staff didn't ask for any evidence of a request from the owners and she had ready access to the firm's files. Someone led her into the file room and she was astonished at how much paperwork there was. It would probably take days, if not weeks, to wade through the many transactions, and she soon discovered that there were layers of companies and ownerships for the accounts. What she usually considered a bonanza of information had only resulted in confusion and obfuscation and she might have hit a dead end already.

Discouraged, Amanda returned to her office and pondered how to find out more information about the firm when her telephone rang. It was the gas company informing her that they needed to do a meter reading.

"What?" she muttered aloud. "Do they really expect that someone is going to be home every time they want to read the meter?"

Coat and hat back on, she trudged to her car and drove back to her new house to see the meter reader outside in the alley. She introduced herself and asked if it was necessary for someone to be on the premises for the reading.

"Sorry, Miss. I could find the meter behind the smaller dwelling in the back but I need access to the big house, too."

"All right," Amanda said. "Let me get my keys." She was going to have to think of some solution to this. There was no way she could take off work for these inconveniences.

She returned and went to the back gate of the big house and let him in the yard. She looked back at the house and saw that someone was inside and, once the workman had finished, she knocked on the back door and entered the kitchen.

"Shirley, is that you?" she asked, seeing the back of a young woman with shoulder length, dark hair who turned around swiftly in surprise.

"Oh," she said.

"Gretchen. Sorry. You're not at work?"

"No, I have a bad toothache and just made an appointment with the dentist. I came home to put some oil of cloves on it in the meantime."

"Poor you. That's awful."

"Who was that? He rang the doorbell several times and being here by myself, I didn't dare answer."

"That was wise of you. It was the gas company meter reader. I expect he'll be showing up every month. We'll have to figure something out where he can have access without giving him a key to the gate."

Gretchen looked down at her watch. "I'd better get going. I do hate going to the dentist."

"The good thing is that he will probably make the pain go away."

"I'm afraid I may have cracked a tooth," Gretchen said, the same worried look on her face. "If he has to take it out, so be it."

"I'm going back downtown. If his office is there or on the way, I can drop you off."

"Oh, thank you, that would be kind."

During the ride, Amanda tried to calm Gretchen down by asking her questions, but she seemed preoccupied with holding her hand to her cheek and clutching her purse in her lap.

"You and Shirley have known each other a long time?" Amanda asked.

"Yes, for years and years. We grew up together."

"Is that why you both decided to move to Boston?"

"It was Shirley's idea. My father was dead against it, but somehow, he saw that there was little back home in the way of work. And I think he was getting tired of me going on about it. Before we came to your place, Shirley and I were living in a one-bedroom apartment downtown. It was close to work, but your house is so much nicer."

"Thank you. I can understand why you wanted to leave home. This economic situation has simply got to get better. When you're a woman, it's even harder. I had heard that people in high places were discouraging women from working, thinking that we'd take men's jobs."

"That's silly. I can tell you I haven't seen or heard of a man working at a typewriter all day like I do anymore than I'd want to dig a ditch."

"Exactly. I was frustrated at the lack of opportunities."

Gretchen looked over at her. "But you come from a rich family. And you're married."

Amanda felt awkward at having compared herself to the girl.

"Well, not rich," she said, trying to downplay her family's standing. "And I wasn't married when I first started working. In our case, it does mean two incomes, which I don't think many families can swing. But it seems to have worked out so far. Here we are, yes?"

"Thank you, Mrs. Halloran," Gretchen said, looking up at the building as she exited. "I expect I'll be fine," she added in a tone that suggested she wasn't banking on it.

~

BRENDAN AND DOMINIC were busy at the station interviewing the four women who had worked as kitchen staff during the party. Two were employees of the Whitings and were appropriately disturbed by the events at the party, having known Spencer and Bitsy for a few years. Not to mention the thought that the death of the family provider might affect their own future employment.

"Now, Eileen, Sheila, can you tell me how you came to work at the party that night," Brendan asked.

The two women looked at one another and Sheila answered. "Mrs. Whiting asked us if we could assist them at this special event."

Until that moment, neither Brendan nor Dominic had picked up the Irish lilt in her voice. But then again, they had previously answered in monosyllables.

"What were you asked to do?"

"Mrs. Whiting took us to that grand house and had us wash and dry all these plates and glasses that looked like they hadn't been used in years."

"They were a proper mess," Eileen added. "Filthy."

"I gather the man whose house it was lived there alone for many years," Brendan said.

"Poor soul. That explains it."

"What else did you do?"

"Some men came in and moved furniture out of the rooms and Mrs. Whiting asked us to sweep and mop those rooms."

Eileen shook her head. "It was a job, all right."

"And then?"

"The night of the party, one of Mr. Whiting's employees, Reggie, wasn't it?" she asked the other, who nodded. "Drove us back to the house. I must say it looked much better at night, lit up like that, than dusty in the daytime with the motes floating through the air."

"What were you expected to do?"

"Mrs. Whiting had hired people to make up the food and deliver it. We were to keep an eye on the plates and refresh them as needed. Also, we had to wash the used dishes and glasses, if that needed to be done."

"So, you were in and out of the dining room?"

"From time to time. There was a little peephole in the swinging door from the dining room to the kitchen so we could see when the guests had moved out to dance or play games or whatever they were doing. That's when we would go out and clear things away."

"Where did the other two girls come from?"

"Sometimes when the Whitings throw big parties at their house, they hire outside servers from some agency to take the burden off us. They seemed nice enough," Eileen said and Sheila nodded.

"Did you see anything strange during the evening?"

"Aside from the costumes people were wearing? No. People came and went from the big room to the dining room to get a bite to eat or to get a drink from that fella, Randy, at the bar."

"Did you see anyone come from the backyard to the kitchen?"

"Certainly not. It would have scared the daylights out of me if someone had."

"What about from the door that leads into the hallway?"

"No."

"Nor anybody down the back stairs?"

"I didn't know the back stairs were there. Although I'm not surprised. I wouldn't have poked around in any case. It wasn't my place."

"Why did Mr. Whiting ask you to leave the kitchen?"

"Well, he didn't exactly. He asked all four of us to go out and clear up the dirty dishes and glasses, which took some time as people had left them on the floor and window sills around the room."

"Which one of you did that?"

"We all did. When we went back in the kitchen some time later, Connie noticed a door ajar and the light to the basement on. You know the rest."

"Did you hear anything while you were clearing up in the dining room? Like raised voices or a crashing sound?"

They both shook their heads.

"If you think of anything else that might be of use, please don't hesitate to call us," Brendan said, standing and giving each one his card. "Thank you."

When they had left, Dominic said, "You don't think Mr.

Whiting might have gotten fresh with one of the maids who took out their revenge, do you?"

Brendan's dark eyebrow shot up. "Interesting theory. We might have to wait nine months to find out."

"What about Shirley? Did she feel jilted by her boss, do you think?"

"She seems like someone who lands on her feet. If she felt jilted, she recovered pretty quickly by taking up with the other one."

"Oh, these fickle women," Dominic said with a smile. "And we at the mercy of their whims."

"Well, professor, if you could bring in the other two women, perhaps we'll learn something."

The two young women who came in evidently didn't know each other before the evening of the party. The only thing they had in common was having signed up for a temporary agency that asked if they might be interested in working from time to time at a party.

"I made sure to find out if it was *that kind* of a party, if you know what I mean," the blonde girl named Joan said with a twist of her mouth. "And the woman said it wasn't that kind of an agency, so I didn't mind the extra work from time to time."

"Me, neither," said Connie, the smaller girl. "I do waitressing during the week but found out this agency gets calls for special events. Weddings and like that. It never hurts to pick up an extra couple of bucks."

"What did the work entail?"

"Wearing the outfit they gave us and picking up used plates and glasses and bringing them back to the kitchen to get washed. One of the guests thought I was wearing a costume and asked me my name. Then he saw I wasn't wearing a mask and got all confused."

"Did either of you notice anyone coming in the back door to the yard, or the door to the hall or down the back stairs?"

They looked at one another and shook their heads. "Just Mrs. Whiting and her husband at the beginning of the party and then he came in later and shooed us out to pick up more used plates and glasses. I don't know why. We were on top of the work, but you learn to do what you're told."

"And when you came back in you saw the basement door was ajar," Brendan prompted and they both nodded their heads vigorously. "Which one of you…?"

"It was me," Connie said. "How I wish I had never gone over to investigate." She shivered.

"Did you hear anything while you were clearing up in the dining room? Like raised voices or a crashing sound?" Brendan asked.

They both shook their heads.

"If you can remember anything else that might be of use to us, please call," Brendan said, handing each of them his card. The blonde gave him a smile that faded when she saw the wedding band but maintained her poise.

"My question is: why was the door to the basement left ajar? Was someone in a hurry to get away or was it deliberate? To make sure the body was discovered quickly?" Brendan asked Dominic.

"What difference would it make when the body was found? If he had been found later, we would still be in a muddle of who was where and when."

"I for one, have had enough of today. Dinner at the Burnsides tonight," Brendan said.

"Sounds good. I guess I need to get married sometime soon. I'm tired of eating out."

"I thought your mother insisted you eat at their house?"

"Of course. For two reasons. One, she thinks I'll be poisoned if I eat anywhere else, which is ridiculous, because you know I grab a sandwich whenever I can for lunch. Two, she wants to pump me about why I'm still single. How can I not be single if I have to eat at my parents' house every night. And she's always got a list of eligible girls, daughters of her friends."

"What's wrong with that?"

"I've known these girls since I was a kid. How can I think of someone like that romantically?"

"Give it a try. You never know."

MRS. BURNSIDE WAS in her element hosting her adult daughters and their husbands and glad that she had made them commit to the weekly family get-together.

"So, how has the week been for you all so far?" she asked.

"Busy for me," Louisa said. "We're starting to move into the winter season and all evening gowns and deb balls. The mothers can be quite difficult."

"Whatever do you mean? Was I that way?" her mother asked with a laugh, putting her hand to her chest.

"I should rephrase that. The mothers want one kind of dress. High-necked and full. The daughters want plunging necklines and slinky profiles. The compromise should be something in between but it's a war of words that some people don't mind having in public."

"What a shame," her mother said. "I'm glad you two were not like that."

"That's because we knew it was of no use putting up a fight, Mother," Amanda said.

Simona came into the sitting room and announced that dinner was served, and they proceeded into the dining room with its bow windows that overlooked the back garden.

"And work? How is work, Rob?" Mr. Burnside asked.

"We're getting a lot of interest from managers of various bands to perform. That's fine, but it's time-consuming to audition them to make sure that the tone is right for us. Not too modern and jazzy but not too pokey. Somewhere in between so the band can be background and guests have an opportunity to converse with each other."

"My, that's a tall order," Mr. Burnside said.

"We've had occasions with standout performers and that has attracted a big crowd, but we need to keep a balance between that and creating an atmosphere where people can talk and hear one another. We're not a concert venue, after all."

They sat in their usual places while Mr. Burnside stood to carve the roast beef. "Brendan, how is that new case of yours coming along?"

"Slowly, of course. I'm sure you can imagine how difficult it is to interview the many people who were in the house at the time with almost all of them in costume and masks."

Mrs. Burnside cleared her throat, which Amanda took to mean that she wished the conversation to move on to more pleasant things.

"Let me ask you a question, Daddy. When two people get into a business partnership and one of them dies, who inherits?" Amanda asked.

"That should be very clearly set out in the partnership agreement from the beginning. The remaining partner usually takes over everything."

Amanda looked at Brendan. "Not the deceased person's survivors?"

"Of course not. Can you imagine? My firm has numerous partners. If the contracts were such that family inherited part of the firm—well, think of the chaos. Spouses and multiple children, none of whom know anything about the law getting involved in the day-to-day activities. Usually there is a payout to the family. Of course, it all depends upon how the contract was drawn up. Pass your plate, please, dear," he said to his wife.

Amanda furrowed her brow as she thought about Bitsy. Had she assumed that she was going to get a portion of the real estate business? Or a substantial settlement? Now she knew she had to investigate the original partnership agreement between Hammond and Whiting to see who gained from Spencer's early demise.

Chapter 16

"What are you up to today?" Brendan asked Amanda as he applied butter to his toast.

"By the way, these eggs are great."

"They're just scrambled eggs. And they're probably cold. Cook never would have tolerated serving them like that. Also, she would have made bacon or sausages, but I didn't get up early enough and didn't want to splatter grease even on my apron."

"That's fine. We don't need the three-course breakfasts that they serve at chez Burnside."

"You're just being kind."

"Cook also doesn't have to go to work in a suit and heels, fully made up with hair just so as you do," Brendan said.

"True. She has her uniform and hairnet and I have my uniform."

"Thank goodness you don't have a hairnet. Those things are hideous."

"I'm meeting with Mr. Hammond this morning to ask him about the partnership contract."

"I understand from Clyde that you are now doing some consultation with our department."

"Oops. I did mean to tell you, but things got busy yesterday. It's all on the up and up. He checked and I'm only doing financial and contractual investigations. No conflict of interest and all very safe."

"It would seem so on the face of things, but money and agreements about money are often at the heart of disagreements and worse."

"Pass the marmalade, please," Amanda asked. "True, but I don't think he's going to do anything in his office to endanger my life. And I'll be very oblique in my questions so he might not catch on to what I'm really after."

Brendan cocked his head to one side. "Those wheeler-dealers are always sharper than they appear. He puts on a front as a slightly oblivious Mr. Nice Guy, but I'd be surprised if that wasn't a façade. He didn't get where he is by actually being that."

Amanda put her fork down for a moment. "Do you think he did away with his partner?"

"It did occur to me. But he seemed to have a hard time navigating that costume while he danced. His alibi was that he was holed up in the first-floor bathroom due to something he ate earlier in the day. I'm not sure I believe him."

"He could have come in through the hall door to the kitchen, and no one in the dining room would have seen him. Everyone else was upstairs. Then he could have gone back out the same way once the deed was done."

"Exactly."

Amanda made a face. "No witnesses, of course. I surveyed what documents the bank had and there was so much, it didn't help me at all. It seems there are a bunch of companies that possibly do different things under the umbrella of Hammond & Whiting."

"Or they shuffle money among the various companies as needed."

Amanda looked up. "That sounds complicated to keep track of."

"That's the point. To mask the reality of their transactions. If it's a gain, they might want to portray to their investors or clients that it didn't do so well. If it's a loss, they might want to make the loss look bigger and pocket the difference. The opposite might also be true: hiding a loss by reporting a gain."

"That seems like a big effort. How could anyone keep all that straight? I mean, what is real and what is fantasy?"

Brendan shrugged. "I always wondered about the intricacies of keeping a second set of books. Luckily, I'm not in a business where I'm accountable for the financial success of each encounter I'm involved in."

"Maybe not financial, but surely the Chief has a little tally sheet in a drawer where he keeps tabs on your wins and losses," she said.

"I don't doubt it. But at least he doesn't put a dollar value on it or I'd be up the creek."

"What are you doing today?" she asked him.

"Seeing the Sun and the Moon."

"What? Do you mean you'll be there from morning until night?"

"Not at all. I'm interviewing the couple that came dressed as the Sun and Moon."

Amanda laughed. "What fun."

"And later, the Devil and an Angel are coming in for a chat."

"That man's pointed beard was a brilliant costume touch," Amanda said.

"I looked at him closely—it was real, not painted on."

"Well, I'd better get going," Amanda said, taking her dishes to the sink. "I guess this is for later," she said, glancing at the dirty frying pan. "At least we'll get a square meal this evening."

THE HAMMOND & Whiting offices were bustling with the clack of typewriters and ringing phones when Amanda arrived. She met the impeccably coiffed, dressed and made-up receptionist that Brendan had told her about. While plenty of young women in Boston would envy the young woman's job—public facing, glamorous and certainly not taxing—Amanda thought it must be one of the least interesting office jobs on offer. It required social skills, certainly, and the right accent, but it seemed that once she made her inquiry of who the new arrival was and announced it via the telephone, her task was done until the next guest appeared. During the half hour that Amanda waited, she was the only person in reception.

Mr. Hammond came into the room looking flustered.

"I apologize for keeping you, Miss Burnside. There was quite a mix-up with documents for a complicated transaction that had to be completed today." He had grasped her hand in both of his as he continued to rattle off the difficulties of lost titles and possible missing heirs. "Oh, but you didn't come to hear me complain about the beginning of my workday. My office is this way," he gestured gracefully down a carpeted hallway that was significantly quieter than the rest of the busy office. A secretary sat outside his office and stood as they approached.

"May I get you anything, Mr. Hammond?" she asked.

"No, thank you. This way," he said.

His office was four times the size of the largest partner's office at her father's firm and decorated with modern steel-framed furniture in black and white leather. It was impressively contemporary although Amanda wondered how comfortable it would be. Before she had a chance to sit down, a voice spoke from a far corner of the room.

"Hello, again." It was Shirley, gathering a pile of file folders from a table near the huge floor-to-ceiling windows.

"Hello," Amanda replied.

"I think you've met my assistant," Mr. Hammond said.

"Yes, indeed." Amanda sat down and was relieved when Shirley crossed the room on her way to the exit.

"Remember, the devil is in the details," she murmured as she went by.

Was she being provocative or giving a warning about how the company worked? Amanda settled for the first choice. Shirley was an ambitious young woman and there was no way she would jeopardize her current situation. Whatever that was.

"What can I help you with?" Mr. Hammond asked. He had curiously mobile eyebrows that rose and fell as he spoke and listened, adding a touch of drama to their conversation.

"It's a fairly simple request. Can you detail the nature of your partnership agreement with the late Mr. Whiting?"

"Oh, well," he said, standing up and running his fingers through his hair. "We'd been friends forever and once rivals and then decided that we'd be great as a team."

"I just meant, in light of his passing, who inherits his portion of the business?"

"It was a straight-forward partnership. If one of us decided to leave, we would split the assets and liabilities. Or one of us could buy the other out, if we so chose." He was now pacing the room.

"But what about when one person is deceased?" Amanda asked.

"That's the end of the partnership. That's all."

"Does Mrs. Whiting get his share or is she now a partner?"

Her father had suggested that the partnership going to the widow was unlikely, but she needed to ask.

"No, she is not my partner. The partnership is dissolved and she'll get his share of the assets and liabilities. There were several companies under the umbrella of Hammond & Whiting. Some were wholly owned by me, some wholly owned by him."

"Does she know about this?"

Mr. Hammond sat down again. "I don't really know. I assume that Spencer had informed her of the nature of our partnership and what he owned. I'm sorry to say that some of *his* companies were not doing well. In fact, he was borrowing from Peter to pay Paul, if you get my meaning."

"So, the company wasn't doing as well as everyone said?" Amanda asked.

"Who said? We're doing very well indeed."

"Would you mind if I looked at the property management records at the bank?

Hammond chortled. "That's highly proprietary information, I'm afraid. Investors' money and all that."

Amanda made a crestfallen expression.

"Tell you what, I'll grant you permission to look at the main Hammond & Whiting accounts for the past few months. You'll see that we're in profit. You tell Mr. Richardson at the bank that it's okay by me." He smiled broadly.

"That's good to hear. It seems that Mrs. Whiting is going to have a harder time sorting through all of the paperwork," Amanda said.

"I should think so. She's going to have to hire someone to pick all the pieces apart and I'm afraid it won't be pretty. That beautiful monstrosity of a house may have to go on the market. He had it mortgaged up to the hilt and, knowing Spencer, he might not have told her that. I don't see how she'll be able to maintain the cash flow to keep it." He was matter of fact in his comments, all manner of sympathy gone from his voice.

"That would be a pity."

"Yes. Well, she has a brother who will take her in if need be." He looked at his wristwatch and smiled. "I'm sorry to cut our conversation short, but I really must get back to business." He stood and held out his hand to her and she got up.

"Thank you for your time," Amanda said, seeing a way forward.

BRENDAN HAD NOT FARED WELL in his interview with the Sun and the Moon, a young couple with distant connections to a friend of Louisa's. They were part of the last people invited in an attempt to round out the "thirty under thirty" theme of the costume party and were flattered to be included in the group until they were informed they had to pay for their costumes.

"Where in the world am I going to appear dressed as the Sun in the near future, do you think?" Barton asked, clearly annoyed at the bait and switch. "My photo was in the newspaper, but who knew it was me? That stupid photographer never asked for names, if you can believe it."

"Wasn't that part of the party's game? Not knowing who anyone was behind the mask until the end?" Brendan asked.

"I thought it was a bit presumptuous to assign us costumes in the first place. Although mine was rather pretty with flowing light blue chiffon," Deborah added. Barton shot an annoyed look at her attempt to rescue what he thought was a disastrous evening not of his own making.

"AND THEN THE big shot flings himself down the basement steps! I'm not surprised. He had a terrible reputation."

"We shouldn't speak ill of the dead," Deborah said.

"How can you say that when the man stole a client from me? I almost didn't want to go once I found out whose party it was. But I was intrigued about what he was up to and I was going to talk to him. But I didn't get to. His boots put the party to a quick end," Barton added.

"I know. I was there," Brendan said. "The Wizard."

"How did it happen?" Deborah asked.

"That's what we're trying to find out. Why he was in the basement? Where were you when the sardines game began?"

"I had a hard enough time maneuvering around with that gigantic sun hat thing on my head that I didn't relish trying to find my way in the dark to squat with a lot of people I didn't know until the game was over. I parked myself in a corner of the dining room and nursed a stiff drink."

Deborah rolled her eyes at him. "Well, I thought it was fun while it lasted and joined in watching grown people racing around in the dark and giggling. It reminded me of being a child and playing with my cousins."

"Childish, I'll agree with you on that," Barton said.

"Oh, Chip. Don't be such a grump. Anyway, I was busy peering into the rooms on the second floor when I heard the commotion from downstairs. Several people raced by me to see what was going on. But I couldn't tell you who. It was dim after all and I can't remember what the costumes were supposed to be."

"Were you surprised that you were invited, based on your past history?" Brendan asked Barton.

"No, he was the sort of guy that wanted to rub your nose in a failed sale. And I expected the party would be the last time I would ever speak to the man. Except I didn't get to. And it sure turned out to be that way," Barton said.

"Yes, you said that already," Brendan commented. He thought back on the Sun's costume headpiece and whether he could have removed the headpiece at some point during the evening and made his way into the kitchen through the hallway door. Had there been anyone in the sitting room at the time? No, everyone was either racing around upstairs or drinking in the dining room. And for the life of him, he couldn't remember seeing somebody nursing a drink in the corner.

Noticing Brendan's silence, Barton asked, "Is there anything else?"

"Not just yet. Thank you.

The couple got up and Barton gave Brendan one last irritated look before he opened the door and followed his wife into the corridor.

Chapter 17

"Who were they?" Dominic asked of the two people he passed just outside Brendan's door.

"A mismatched couple if ever I saw one. In terms of the investigation, they were not helpful at all. I do remember their costumes, however. She was Moon, in a flowing blue dress and crescent on her head. The poor guy was Sun and his head looked like a giant sunflower. There's no way he could have moved inconspicuously around the house unless he took the thing off."

"And that was touted as the party of the year?"

"I suppose it ended up being memorable, at least."

"By the way, Devil and Angel are waiting in the lobby. Shall I bring them in?"

"Yes, thanks and stay for the interview if you don't have anything else to do."

"Me? Busy? Don't be silly," Dominic said.

The Devil and Angel were the next two people to be ushered into the conference room, the man still sporting the trimmed mustache and beard that made his costume so memorable. His companion with her fluffy blonde hair and pale skin was the perfect Angel.

"Thank you for coming in. Your names, please?" Brendan said, looking at the guest list for reference.

"Carla Johnson," the woman said.

"Bill Williams," the man said.

Brendan looked up for a moment.

"Third most common name in the census," he clarified.

"How did you come to be invited to the party that night?"

"I heard about it through one of the band members. He said the hostess was at her wit's end getting enough people to fill out the thirty she had in mind. We were latecomers, so to speak."

"At least we didn't have to pay for our costumes. I heard the other folks did."

"That's true," Brendan said, irked that he and Amanda were one of the couples that had to pay for their attendance.

"Can you tell me anything unusual that you may have witnessed?"

They looked at one another. The man spoke first.

"Nothing really. It was an odd party. They wanted everyone to keep their masks on as it was part of a guessing game at the end: who could figure out who everyone was. In our case, we didn't know anybody except the piano player and he wasn't in the game. It was strange trying to make conversation with people you didn't know and yet not asking questions that could give away their identity. Not that we would know who they were anyway." Bill shook his head at the absurdity of it.

"I guess that's why Bitsy had devised those games. To keep people distracted and engaged."

"If you say so."

"Did you participate in the sardines game?" Brendan asked.

"Sure. We went upstairs together. Carefully, because it was dark. Lots of folks were dashing from room to room. We just walked quietly through each room listening for what we thought were whispers, but wherever she had hidden, she was very quiet."

"Where were you when the shouting began?"

"I suggested we go up to the third floor," Bill said. "Mr. Whiting didn't show us what was up there, so I suspected that might be where she was hiding. Of course, we came back down immediately."

"Had you ever met Mr. Whiting?"

They looked at one another again and shook their heads.

"Not before that evening," Bill said.

"If you think of anything else, please let me know," Brendan concluded, standing and handing a card to each of them. "And thank you." He shook hands with both and Dominic escorted them back to the lobby.

Brendan looked at his watch and walked back to his office. How had the entire day gone by so quickly? His neck and shoulders were tight and he was anxious to get home. Hat on and one arm through his overcoat, Clyde Owens knocked on the open door.

"What have you got?" he asked.

"Nothing more than what we already know. That small piece of fringe in his hand could have come from any one of the costumes that evening. And we have no way of tracking down all those outfits since people seemed to have paid for them out of pocket and may have tossed them out already."

"We have a list of the guests and we haven't even begun to ask for them. Some guests seem to have been from out of town, some with very little connection to the Whitings, like the last couple we had in. Peter Pan and Wendy have disappeared, along with the Indian Chief and the Princess, Holmes and Watson and the Strongman and the Bareback Rider," Brendan said.

"Do you want me to contact Mrs. Whiting and see if we can figure out where to contact those people?"

"Clyde, that would be a tremendous help. And as they say, tomorrow is another day."

BRENDAN ARRIVED HOME, relieved that his day was over, to find Amanda at the dining room table sifting through paperwork. She lifted her head.

"Hello!"

He came up behind her and put his arms around her shoulders. "I hope that's not work," he said.

"I'm afraid so."

He took off his coat and hat and went to the sideboard. "It's cocktail time, dear."

"Now that sounds good. I could use a break. Was work so difficult today?"

"No, just one dead end after another. What can you expect from a houseful of people in costumes running around in the dark? And, of course, nobody saw anything."

"That familiar phrase."

"How would you like a Manhattan?"

"Very much," Amanda said.

"Do we have cherries?" he asked.

"Of course. What proper household doesn't?" She went to the kitchen to retrieve a small jar from the refrigerator. "Why do we put sweet cherries in drinks and then bitters, and what the heck are bitters?" she called out.

"I'll read the label and try to find out," Brendan said. "Hmm," he muttered. "Herbs and botanicals. Family secret. That doesn't help. I've read that slightly alcoholic drinks with strong herbs are taken in Europe for health reasons."

Amanda had come back into the room, sniffed at the bottle of bitters and wrinkled her nose. "I guess that was so the patient would say they were better in order not to have to take it again. A dash of that stuff is supposed to make a

Manhattan what it is, but can you imagine a whole glass of it?"

"There's something in Hungary called Unicum that people drink for health reasons. Once again, family secret."

"I've brought some ice," Amanda said.

"Good woman," he said, leaning over to kiss her. He took the ice from the bowl she handed him, put it in the cocktail shaker, added whiskey, vermouth and a dash of bitters before putting another container on top and shaking to chill the drink. He strained it into two glasses. "Thank you, Rob and Louisa, for the cocktail apparatus and the complement of alcohols," he said, pointing to the well-equipped sideboard.

Amanda plopped a cherry in each glass; they toasted and retreated to the living room couch.

"Brendan, I've found the most interesting information."

"Please, you're not going to plague me with work issues. I'm off the clock."

"I happen to know that you're not ever entirely off the clock. So, digging back into my notes from the bank, the thing I found strange was the number of companies that were listed under Hammond & Whiting, probably relating to individual properties, and how frequently money was transferred from one company to another. It would take me a month to draw a map of what went where. I'm starting to wonder if even the two men knew what was going where and when."

"Who was in charge of the financial end?"

"It appears it was Mr. Hammond. From what I saw, his initials were on the paperwork. I assumed that Spencer knew of those transactions, but perhaps he didn't."

"I thought that Spencer was the 'rainmaker', as the expression goes, the person who got the clients and closed the deal. That would make Hammond the record keeper, especially if Spencer wasn't a detail-oriented person and trusted his partner implicitly."

"I have two questions. Were they managing the properties of other people or were these companies solely their own? You know, an account for one rental unit, a separate account for another and so on. Was all this juggling of funds legitimate? Were they funneling money from clients' properties into their own account? Were they trying to cover something up? It would take someone a long time to sort through the trail of paperwork. Time that I don't have. And permission that I don't have, either. And I also don't have the expertise to know if what they were doing with clients' funds was appropriate."

"We can probably find someone to look into that if you think it's necessary."

"This Manhattan is very good, but we'd better drink up or we'll be late."

"For what?"

"Dinner with the girls, of course."

Brendan groaned.

"Come on, think of it this way. We get expertly cooked food and we don't have to do the cleanup. If I were preparing the meals, I would have to do the grocery shopping after work. Then I would come home and probably burn the food. Neither of us would be happy with that situation."

"And as a result, what?" he asked playfully.

"Either we'd need to get divorced or eat out every night," she said.

"It would be expensive to eat out every night, but perhaps worth the money."

"Come on," she said, taking his hand and pulling him up from the couch.

"It's just that the conversation is not that stimulating, if you know what I mean."

"Then it's up to us to lead it in a different direction, away from clothing and gossip."

Brendan groaned again.

"Please stop making that noise," she said, reaching for her overcoat.

They walked the short distance across the yard and up the back steps to the main house, entering through the kitchen.

"Good evening, Mrs. O'Reilly," Amanda said to the woman arranging a salad on a plate.

"Good evening. Pork chops and mashed potatoes tonight. The girls are in the sitting room," she added.

They made their way through the dining room, its table set for five, and Amanda looked over at Brendan.

"You think they've voted me out?" he whispered.

"Not a chance," she whispered back. Then louder as they walked into the sitting room, "Good evening, ladies."

The four young women chimed back their greeting in unison.

Shirley got up as they came in, her coat over her arm. "Sorry, I won't be joining you this evening." She put her coat on and smiled. "How was your conversation with the prodigal son?" she asked slyly.

The couple looked at one another befuddled.

"Mister *Williams*," she said for emphasis and went to the front door just as the doorbell rang. She turned. "I told you the devil was in the details."

Brendan shut his eyes in frustration and turned away to hide his embarrassment.

Puzzled by the remark, Amanda put on a smile and said, "I believe dinner is ready."

She turned to Brendan with a look.

"I'll tell you later," he said. "Please, ladies. After you," he gestured.

"I'm sorry Shirley is missing out on this wonderful meal," Amanda said once they were all seated and the platters brought in from the kitchen.

"I'm not. More for me," Dassie said.

"Where's she gone?" Rebecca asked.

"She's out with Mr. Hammond," Gretchen said, looking abandoned.

"This week," Dassie added with a giggle.

"That's not nice," Gretchen said.

"Just observing. That's all. I didn't tell the girls yet, but today, guess who came into the store?"

They shook their heads.

"Eddie Cantor!"

The room burst with sounds of disbelief and surprise.

"He's in town performing somewhere for a few nights. Isn't that exciting?"

"Did you get to talk to him?" Rebecca asked.

"Gosh, no. He came in and stopped right in the middle of the first floor, put his finger to the side of his face as if trying to remember what he came in for. Of course, by that time, everyone had stopped in their tracks and were staring at him."

"Are you sure it was him?"

"Do you know of anyone else who looks like that? The big eyes, the slicked back hair, expensive suit, although he was a lot shorter than I imagined."

"Of course. You've seen him on a big screen in a movie theater. Everybody looks big."

That got a laugh from everyone.

"He went to the men's section on the second floor. I wish I had thought to get his autograph or something," Dassie added.

"What for?" Rebecca asked.

"I don't know. Isn't that what you're supposed to do when you meet famous people? I guess you start a collection.

Maybe I need to get an autograph book like the ones we had in school."

"Good luck finding famous people in Boston."

"Maybe we have some famous criminals. What do you think, Mr. Halloran?"

Brendan ignored the question.

"Pass the salad, please," Amanda asked. "Mrs. O'Reilly is spoiling me and I don't care. Cooking is an art, but she also does the meal planning and purchasing. She must know a very good butcher."

"I hate to bring up business," Rebecca said, "but I'd like to know if you would offer a reduction in rent if we were to choose to eat out some meals."

The question took Amanda by surprise and she felt she had to stall. "You get Monday through Friday meals now and weekends on your own. I wouldn't like to start to make exceptions because that would throw the meal planning into chaos. Like this evening, for example."

"I only ask as a matter of interest. It seems to me that Shirley won't be taking meals much with us in the near future."

Gretchen shot her a dirty look. "What do you mean?"

"Read the writing on the wall, dear. As hard as she's working for it, she'll fly the coop any day now." At that, Rebecca waggled the fingers on her left hand flashing her own ring finger with its small engagement diamond.

Chapter 18

"I can't believe I didn't catch that!" Brendan said to Dominic the next morning. "He had me from the get-go by saying Williams was the third most common name in the United States. Brilliant. Threw me off."

"Are you sure he's the estranged son?"

"I'll bet you lunch that he is."

"I'm not taking the bet. I'll find his number and get him back in here. Then we'll find out."

"Is there even a photo of the man anywhere? High school or college photo?" Brendan asked.

"Do you know if he even went to high school or college here?"

Brendan slammed the newspaper he had in his hand onto the desk. "Of course not. I feel I'm being manipulated from all sides."

"I'm going to get some coffee," Dominic said, not adding, "until you calm down." But he had never seen Brendan so frustrated and didn't want to add fuel to the fire.

Two more people were scheduled to come in, and they were on time and nervous at the prospect of being involved in a police investigation.

"You're the Griffins?" Brendan asked.

"Yes, George and Julia."

"Please sit down," he said, watching George take in his surroundings.

"How do you know the Whitings?"

"Gosh, I went to school with Spencer. Prep school. I've known him forever." He stopped himself. "Best man at his wedding and all. This is so horrible."

"Yes, it always is," Brendan said, before reminding himself not to be so curt with people.

"What was he like?"

"Spence? Full of life. Bursting with ideas for fun things to do, people to meet, always on the go. Like a whirling dervish."

"And you know Bitsy, of course."

"Oh, yes, she was the stabilizing force in his life. You wouldn't think it, but behind that tiny frame and sweet face is a stalwart person. If she were a man, she'd be a warrior."

"Really, George," his wife said, reacting to his exaggeration.

"What happens now?" Brendan asked.

The couple looked at each other, searching for an answer.

"I suppose she'll sell that ridiculous house and move in with her brother. I don't know what she'll be able to pull out of the business with Hammond."

"You knew him in school, too, isn't that right?"

"Yes. Howard loved being in Spencer's wake, so to speak. He was much more serious about school, grades and so on. His family had experienced some financial problems even before the Crash and I guess he didn't want to find himself in that situation. He was always focused on creating a solid future for himself. Spencer—well, he figured everything was going to fall into his lap somehow."

"Interesting partnership then, wouldn't you say?"

"Opposites attract," Julia said.

"I'm guessing that, since you were invited to the party, you continued socializing with the Whitings over time."

"Yes, quite frequently," Julia said.

"How would you describe their marriage?"

Julia pulled her head back and looked at her husband and back to Brendan. "What do you mean?"

"I mean, did they seem happy? Compatible? Or did they like to fight?"

"No, no fighting, ever," Julia said. "Spencer liked to overdo everything and Bitsy was there to pull him back to reality." She stared at Brendan as if challenging him to go deeper.

"So, the night of the party, when the sardines game began, where were you two?"

"Scouring the second floor, going into every room and listening for any telltale murmur or movement. We were the first to find her. I don't know why, but it was a relief to squash in with her and have a moment's peace. Naturally we didn't talk. She just wrinkled her nose at me in annoyance that she had been found so quickly. It was some time before Cleopatra made her entrance, pulling up the cloth and staring at us in the darkness as if not sure she was seeing three people or had just imagined it. She squeezed in without a word and sat well away from us."

"That's because your ridiculous wolf costume was shedding. I'm surprised one of us didn't sneeze and give the hiding place away," Julia said.

"We could hear people coming into the room, looking around, talking and then leaving. Most of the seekers seemed intent on peering into the closet at the other end of the room. Then the Queen and the Witch found us and came in under the cloth. I couldn't imagine how many more people we could possibly fit."

"How long would you say you were there before you heard someone cry out?"

George looked at his wife and shrugged. "I don't know. Ten minutes maybe?"

"I'd say a bit more than that. Maybe it seemed like it because it was dusty and stuffy. And, of course, we couldn't talk and give away the game," Julia said. "When I got home, I saw that the whole back of my red riding hood was covered in dust." She shook her head.

"Can you think of any reason someone would want to harm Spencer Whiting?"

George paused before saying, "Well, you know…"

Brendan held his gaze steady on the man.

"Business deals and so forth," he managed to say.

"Such as?"

"Not everyone is happy with the outcome of a transaction. As jolly as Spencer could be, he could also be a steamroller when it came to closing a deal. Making last-minute changes that the other party wasn't anticipating and it being too late to back out."

"I imagine someone might be rather upset to be treated like that."

George chuckled. "Some guy came up to him at the club last week and started chewing him out. He wasn't a member and the staff chucked him out on his ear. Can you imagine?"

Brendan could certainly imagine the scene and George finding it somewhat amusing as well. As if anything goes in business.

"What do you do for a living?" Brendan asked.

"We do real estate appraisals. You know, what the bank expects before they grant a loan or a buyer enters a sales contract."

"Is business good these days?"

"Oh, yes. It's picked up nicely. Actually, it's my father's business and we've expanded into commercial appraisals.

That has significantly expanded our reach in the community."

"I expect you worked with Spencer quite a bit," Brendan said, looking down at his notebook.

"Of course. But it's Howard Hammond who handles the nuts and bolts. Still, I'll miss Spencer tremendously," he added, putting on a sad face.

"If there is anything else you can think of, not just the night of the party, but events in the recent or distant past that might have a bearing on this, please contact me." Once again, he handed over a business card, although he was certain that, if George knew something else in Spencer's past, he wasn't about to reveal it. The way Julia avoided eye contact at that moment confirmed his suspicions.

They had scarcely left when Dominic put his head around the corner and said, "Bill Williams is here."

"Very good. Bring him back."

Brendan fully expected the young man to be contrite after not revealing his connection to the former owner of the house where the party took place, but he was mistaken. Instead, he came into the interview room with an air of confidence and almost a smirk on his face. Before he had a chance to sit down, Brendan asked, "Why didn't you tell me who you were?"

"I did. Bill Williams is my name."

"And was the late Mr. Williams your father?"

"Yes, he was." The man sat down.

"Someone told me the two of you were estranged."

"That's correct. He was a man who possessed nineteenth century viewpoints."

"I imagine he must have been born in the last century. That's not so unusual."

"I understand. But his idea of a parental relationship was, 'do as I say, not as I do.'"

"What did he do that didn't agree with you?"

The cocky veneer was replaced by an impassioned tone. "He was horrible to my mother. He married *below* his class and never let her forget it. He demeaned her and marginalized her to the point that she was a shell. Then he had her institutionalized for good measure."

"That sounds terrible."

"It was appalling. I've never forgiven him. He acted as if nothing were the matter and then he started to 'mold' me, as he put it. The last thing I wanted was to become the heartless man he was. And I told him so. That's when he booted me out and cut me off."

"How long ago was that?"

"About eight years ago. I went out West to get as far away from him as possible. Kicked around in various jobs, not making a fortune, but getting by. I read the out-of-town newspapers at the library and saw the obituary notice but was too late for the funeral. It was held at a church—what a joke! The man not only never attended while I lived with him, but he also violated every possible tenet of the Christian faith."

"Those are strong words."

"I'll modify them. He probably never killed anybody outright, but I'm sure my mother's early death lies at his door."

Brendan was jotting down 'Williams' wife' with the intention of following up with the man's story, if there was anything to be found.

"His beyond-the-grave behavior pushed me to challenge the will in court. It was refused, as I expected, but I intend to appeal."

"My question is, what were you doing at that party? How did you manage to get an invitation?"

"My date was an old friend of mine and somehow the hosts were trying to fill out the guest list. I knew Bitsy, of course, but I had grown this beard and mustache since I last saw her, so I gave her a false name. We used to play as kids but, after all these years, she didn't recognize me."

"What were you hoping to achieve?"

"I'm not sure. I wanted to see the place again. It was just as empty and stark as it felt when it was full of furniture. My father's presence cast a pall on the party."

"Did you know Spencer Whiting?"

"No, I hadn't met him until the party. He paid no attention to me or my date."

"You didn't have a conversation?"

"Not at all. He was busy orchestrating some deal while Bitsy was doling out the instructions to the games."

"What deal?"

"I don't know. He was talking to the guy dressed as Caesar in a side room at one point. What you might call an animated conversation."

"This is the first I've heard of such a conversation."

"As I said, they were in a side room. I was on my way to the bathroom and I heard raised voices. I peered around the corner and heard them."

"What was it about?"

"I couldn't tell. They just seemed to disagree about something. Anyway, I was washing up in the bathroom and someone was knocking furiously on the door. When I opened it, it was that guy in the toga, saying he was going to be sick. He strong-armed me out of the way and I got out of there fast. I didn't want to catch what he might have."

Brendan had felt that portion of Hammond's tale about feeling sick had seemed conveniently manufactured, but now there was some degree of corroboration.

"Where were you when the sardines game began?"

"My date and I trooped upstairs like the good guests we were, and it was chilling to see the rooms bereft of furniture, sheets over the furniture, dust on the floor. I have to admit that I wasn't very enthused about participating and was going to leave the party early. Nobody would have noticed. And then that scream." He shuddered.

"What did you do?"

"Like everyone else, it seems, we went back downstairs immediately and could still hear the noise coming from the kitchen. Then there was chaos with people trying to get into the kitchen to see what the matter was—well, you were there."

"Yes, chaos is a good description."

"When your men got there, I told them that I hadn't seen or heard anything unusual, which is true. Except I had forgotten that conversation I overheard. Perhaps I didn't think it was of any importance."

"It might have been of great importance," Brendan said, making a note to talk to Hammond again.

The last interview that day was with Bitsy's brother, Bruce, and his wife. They came in dressed in black, as was expected, but they seemed more put out by having to deal with a widow in their house than sad for her new situation.

"I'm sorry to have to speak with you again, but there is a lot I don't understand."

"Neither do we," Bruce said. "Such as why Spencer decided to go down into the basement after clearly telling everyone else not to."

"Unless he was planning on meeting someone and didn't want to be interrupted," Sue suggested.

Brendan always found it interesting when people who were brought in for an interview decided that they had to play detective and tried to hide something.

"How is Bitsy doing, by the way?" Brendan asked.

"Taking it like a champ. That's her way. She'll be meeting with their lawyer to discuss next steps."

"Like selling that huge house," Sue said, shaking her head.

"Will she be living with you then?"

Sue looked over at Bruce, who said, "We haven't got to that discussion yet. For now, however, she is staying with us. I expect that she'll be receiving a significant settlement from Hammond & Whiting."

Although Brendan suspected otherwise, he said nothing. That would be their problem to figure out.

"Did you sense any difficulties between them?"

"Are you suggesting that my sister connived to kill Spencer?" Bruce asked, his back up.

"Not at all. I am simply trying to get a feeling about their relationship."

"He thought he was the boss," Sue said. "Although he was mostly hot air. I'll give it to Bitsy—she handled him expertly, allowing him to think he got his way while steering the ship." She smiled.

"The only thing she didn't succeed in doing was limiting his outrageous spending habits. That house, for example. He had to have the top architect and the top decorator. And so many bedrooms you'd think he was operating a hotel or expecting to have six children."

"I suppose if you're in high-end real estate, you've got to impress people with the home you live in," Brendan said.

"True," Spencer's brother-in-law reluctantly agreed. "But not if you've got a huge mortgage on it."

"How do you know that?"

Bruce realized he had probably spoken out of turn and pursed his lips. "Look, Boston is a big city but in certain circles, it's a small town. And when you're dealing daily with the same folks in business and pleasure, sometimes a bit of information slips out."

"As it did just now," Brendan said, at once wondering what motivation the brother-in-law had in doing so.

"You didn't hear it from me," Bruce said quickly. "A glimpse into his bank records will show the same thing."

"We've already done that," Brendan said. It wasn't entirely true; Amanda had looked into the business records, not the individual bank accounts of each of the principals. But he liked to keep folks he interviewed on their toes.

"Is there anything else you'd like to share?" he asked.

"I think we've said enough," Sue said, shooting a look at her husband.

As soon as they left, Brendan went to his office and got on the phone to Amanda, who was back in her office.

"Is there any way you can take a peek at Spencer's personal bank account? And while you're at it, Howard Hammond's?"

"I may be stretching my luck doing that. The bank will probably want written authorization from the family. In any case, it's probably going to have to wait until Monday."

Amanda tried her best to think of some way to get access to documents for both Spencer Whiting and Howard Hammond, but between its being Friday and edging toward three o'clock closing, she was not successful. It would simply have to wait for Monday. Rather than go back to her office, she called it a day and relished having the house to herself for a few hours.

Chapter 19

Amanda stopped at the front door and put her briefcase on the porch bench until she found her key in her handbag. Although she appreciated having a home of her own, she was a bit disappointed that it still didn't look the way she had imagined it. They had unpacked their things long ago, but the mixture of the furniture which had come with the acquisition of the house and the meager items from Brendan's duplex gave a cluttered and disorganized look to the place. Although the living room was large enough, the dark wallpaper and the shade from the tall trees outside made it a gloomy space. She had purchased two interior design magazines—each as pricey as the homes pictured within its pages. Mulling over the photos, she could see that the addition of a mirror over the fireplace could reflect what light came in and the elimination of the wallpaper would brighten the room considerably. Naturally, the rooms in the magazines were all modern with steel and glass, which would look ridiculous in this space. But painting the walls a cream color would make a big difference. And then she thought about the heavy curtains, which certainly kept the warmth in the room but didn't need to be that fusty dark green brocade.

Lost in daydreaming about what the room was going to look like, she was startled by the telephone ringing.

On the other end of the line was a breathless female voice.

"Mrs. Halloran, I hate to bother you, but the faucet upstairs must be broken. I tried turning it off, but the water keeps coming out."

"I'll be right over," Amanda said and hustled back into her shoes and out the door.

When she got inside and upstairs, it was Dassie who awaited her on the landing.

"I'm so sorry, I hope I didn't break anything," she said.

Amanda tried to shut off the faucet with the handle but clearly something was broken. Then she remembered seeing Brendan look under the sink in his apartment when something was amiss. She parted the cloth curtains that surrounded the sink and found two knobs, corresponding to the hot and the cold taps above. With some effort, she was able to turn the cold knob to the right and the flow stopped.

"Thank you, Mrs. Halloran. I'm so sorry. I didn't do anything unusual, it just kind of kept going."

"Don't worry. I'm sure it's fixable. But probably not this afternoon and maybe not until Monday, when we can get a plumber in. Perhaps my husband can fix it, I'll ask him when he gets back. It's a good thing you were here when it happened and that I was at home." Amanda got up from her kneeling position and looked out into the hall to see that Gretchen's door was closed.

"Is Gretchen home sick?" she asked.

"I don't know. I only got home a little while ago myself."

Amanda walked to the door and tapped on it. Getting no answer, she knocked. Still no answer and she opened the door to be greeted by a gust of hot air.

"What is going on? Why is there a heater in here? And on full blast?"

"Gretchen was the last to sign on the lease, and the room she got was formerly the upstairs porch that was enclosed. It's not connected to the steam heat so she uses that gas heater."

"Turn it off, please," Amanda said and went to the two sash windows and threw them open to let in the chilly air.

She then turned her attention to the bed where Gretchen lay on her side very still.

"Oh, no!" Amanda shouted. She pulled the coverlet back from Gretchen's face which was slightly flushed and slapped her forcefully on the back. "Wake up! Wake up!" Then to Dassie she said, "Call the police."

"I don't know the number."

"Here, let's pull her out to the hallway," Between the two of them, they dragged the young woman out to the landing. "Keep trying to wake her," Amanda said. "I'll call." She knew the number well enough.

"Help, I need an ambulance. I think someone may have

inhaled deadly gas," she said. She confirmed the address and hung up the upstairs phone extension.

Gretchen had begun to stir and held her head with a groan. A moment later, she vomited.

"Dassie, go downstairs and wait outside the front door so the ambulance people can see which house it is." The young woman stormed down the stairs and out the front door, leaving it wide open.

"Sorry," Gretchen said, seeing the mess on the wooden floor. "I don't know what happened."

"I think you left the heater on high for too long."

"No, I didn't. I remember my father told me not to sleep with the heater on. I came home from work early with cramps and thought I'd take a nap. I'm sure I didn't turn on the heater."

"Don't worry, we'll get you taken care of," Amanda said as Gretchen heaved again.

It wasn't that long a wait but it seemed like an eternity before two ambulance attendants with their stretcher came up the stairs, preceded by Dassie, who pointed toward the patient.

"Oh, she's alive! And breathing!" she said near to tears.

The attendants were swift in placing Gretchen onto the stretcher and transporting her down the stairs.

"What hospital?" Amanda called out to them.

"Mercy," one replied.

It was a place she knew well, since she had worked for the hospital administration first as a volunteer and then as an employee. That was until the Board had a change of heart and the Director she had worked with so well left. As she had shortly thereafter. She knew many of the medical staff, however, and she knew Gretchen would be in good hands.

Once the ambulance had driven away, Dassie collapsed on the sitting room sofa to heaving sobs. Amanda sat next to her and said, "I think you saved her life."

"How horrible that accidents can happen so quickly."

They heard the back door open and close and Mrs. O'Reilly came through, still in her hat and coat.

"What's going on?"

Amanda gave her a summary of the events and the cook shook her head in disbelief. "Let me get out of my coat, and I'll help you clean up."

Minutes later, Amanda and Mrs. O'Reilly, who brought a bucket, mop and cloths in, proceeded to the landing where Gretchen had been sick.

"It's not what I think it is, is it?" the cook asked.

"If you mean, is she pregnant, I don't think so. The gas heater was on high and I think the air became unhealthy as a result."

"That's awful, but better than the alternative," she commented. Once they had cleaned up the hall, they both went back into Gretchen's room to see the curtains fluttering in the stiff breeze that had come up.

"Let's get these closed," Amanda said, shutting one window while the cook tackled the other.

Mrs. O'Reilly looked over at the closet door, which was partially open and tutted. "These girls are messy when they live by themselves. Just look at that," she said holding up what looked like a white sheet, crumpled into a ball, covered with dust and dirt. "Now what do you suppose that is?" she said, pushing it back into the recesses of the closet.

Amanda stood stock still. It all came together in a moment of flashbacks of scenes of the party and she thought she knew exactly what it might mean.

Brendan must have seen the ambulance leaving and, after checking their own dwelling, rushed over to the big house, calling out to see if anyone was there. Dassie was still on the sofa, wiping her eyes and looking lost.

"What's going on?" he asked.

"There's been a bit of an accident," she said.

"Bren? Is that you?" Amanda called from upstairs.

He bounded up the steps two at a time to see her and Mrs. O'Reilly stuffing cloths into a pail.

"Someone was sick," Amanda said.

"Sick enough for an ambulance?"

"The gas heater was on quite high in her bedroom. We'd better chuck it out lest she use it again. First, though, I want to go the hospital and check up on Gretchen."

"Sure, I'll drive," he said.

"I'll just clean up and get my coat," she said, heading down the stairs to get her coat.

WHILE SHE WASHED her hands thoroughly in their own kitchen, Brendan peppered her with questions.

"I don't know when she came home. She said she had cramps and lay down. She insisted she didn't turn the heater on. Let's not badger her too much. What's done is done."

They rode in silence until Amanda finally shared her worries.

"Maybe buying that old house was a complete mistake. You jokingly thought I would be acting like a housemother and that's exactly how I feel right now."

"Did Dassie call you over? What was she doing home so early?"

"She called me about a leaky faucet. Thank goodness I was home and went over. Who knows when anyone else might have discovered Gretchen? Do you think we can somehow get heating into that bedroom? Are we just going to be pouring money into that place forever?"

"It's called home ownership. And yes, we'll be maintaining the house and making improvements as needed. By the way, a roof doesn't last forever, you know."

"Oh," she groaned. "I hadn't even thought of that."

"The sensible thing to do is to set aside money each month for what you might call capital improvements so the cash is there when we need it. It will be healthier psychologically for us instead of reacting to any repair needed as a disaster."

Amanda gave it some consideration. "I think that's a good idea. After all, at some point, we're going to move into the big house and rent out the little one."

"Yes, when we fill ours with lots of children," he said, patting her hand.

"Let's go slowly on the 'lots' for right now. We've got tenants who need us and maybe a parent who needs to be informed of what just happened.

Chapter 20

The story got more complicated with every telling the next day. Gretchen did feel ill at work and her old hometown friend accompanied her home before going back to the office for the remaining hours of the workday. Shirley claimed that Gretchen asked her to turn on the heater before she left, which the other young woman couldn't remember having said. How the heater got turned up to maximum was something that puzzled everyone and then frightened them after the doctor told them that type of the heater could leak carbon monoxide, which could have killed her. Gretchen professed to holding no grudges and Shirley agreed not to tell her friend's family about the incident although Amanda was conflicted about whether she should take it upon herself to do so.

Amanda took the event seriously and asked her father-in-law to come by and check out the heating, plumbing and electrical circuits in both the houses to prevent another disaster. Saturday seemed like the best day for both.

"It's a beautiful place, to be sure," he said, having only been in their home and not the big house. Although not a contractor, he had years of experience with rentals and home repairs and after a few hours of testing and observation he claimed it appeared everything seemed to be up to code.

"That doesn't mean that you might not want to make upgrades as the years go by. They're always thinking of new safety measures. As to the leak upstairs, I think all it needs is a washer and I've got one in my toolbox." He went out to his car and came back with a wrench, a screwdriver and a small box full of round objects. Amanda watched him take the faucet apart and pull out a thin piece of ragged rubber.

"Many years of wear will be fixed in a few minutes." True to his word, he installed it, put the handle back on and then connected the cold water underneath the sink. "Give it a whirl," he said.

"Thank you," Amanda said, appreciating that it turned on and off easily.

"Brendan could have done it just as quickly if he weren't in the middle of a case just now," his father said.

"Yes, and I suppose it wouldn't hurt if I were to learn a few simple repairs."

He gave her the same intense look under dark eyebrows that Brendan would have if he had been there. "There's no need for you to be doing men's work when you've got family to do it."

"That's probably just as well. I might have made a broken faucet into a fountain up to the ceiling instead."

Although it was a Saturday, Brendan was back at work; his first task was talking to Howard Hammond again. He didn't have the advantage of seeing any of the financial records firsthand—and would have to wait for more details after Monday. But he had enough questions to put forth to the man.

Hammond told him that Saturday mornings were devoted to tennis at his club and invited Brendan to meet him at eleven when he expected he'd be done.

The Boston Athletic Association, or B.A.A. as most people referred to it, had been an institution since the last century and, as such, was particular about its membership. Brendan was glad that Hammond hadn't asked him to join him in a match since it had been some time since he had picked up a racquet and it wasn't his favorite form of recreation. He pondered that, twenty years earlier, they wouldn't even have let an Irish American like him in the front door. True to his expectation, it had the aura of a men's club minus the cigar smoke but with a slight whiff of chlorine from an indoor pool somewhere in the building. He hadn't thought of it before, but the tennis courts were indoor as well, a blessing in Boston's inclement weather.

The building at the corner of Exeter and Blagden Streets took up most of the block. There was a constant stream of members entering either to sit in a steam bath, engage in some sport or even eat in their well-appointed dining room. Brendan announced himself at the front desk and was asked to sit in an adjacent room after handing over his hat and coat. It wasn't more than ten minutes before Howard Hammond found him, his face pink with the exertion of a recent game, newly showered and dressed in what passed for a gentleman's casual clothes.

"Nice to see you again. I know it's early, but would you like to join me in lunch?"

"Thank you, no. I just had a few questions that were nagging at me."

Hammond sat down and a waiter appeared, asking what the gentlemen would like to drink.

"Orange juice," Brendan said.

"Very healthful. Same here."

"I think I may have asked you before if Spencer had any enemies."

"Yes, you did. And no, I couldn't point to anyone. He was a big, blustery fellow, which is why everyone took what he said with a grain of salt. But I don't know of anyone who would have wished him harm."

"I had heard that his house was heavily mortgaged," Brendan said.

"I don't know the exact figure, but I'm guessing it was significant. He did like to live big."

"I'm curious about your business relationship. Didn't you say that he brought in the clients and you were the numbers man?"

The waiter came back with two glasses on a tray. After a taste, Brendan knew it had been freshly squeezed and he was glad of his choice. Hammond paused until the waiter was gone before resuming the conversation.

"Yes, that's true."

"Would you say yours was a fifty-fifty type of partnership?"

"In what sense?"

"I haven't got clear on what belonged to the partnership and what your separate properties were."

Hammond gave him a hard look. "Have you been rummaging through my banking details?"

"No, I have not," Brendan answered truthfully, since it was Amanda who had taken on that task and he didn't know if Hammond was aware of their marriage.

"There is a lot of gossip in the business world, you know. And the more successful you are, the more vicious the tales. We had a harmonious relationship and I am sorry it came to a tragic end. I hope you will do your best to find out who perpetrated this vile deed. It will mean a lot to Bitsy as well as to me and all the employees."

"I'll do my best, of course," Brendan said, sensing the interview was coming to an end.

Both men finished their juice, shook hands and Hammond left the room with Brendan no wiser than when the conversation began except that he noted how the other man had dodged questions so easily.

When he got home, he found his father was still there having coffee with Amanda.

"I hope you're not working seven days a week, Son," Mr. Halloran said.

"Not if I can help it. But there are so many strange things about this case and an awful lot of people involved. I might not get to the bottom of it for some time."

"Don't throw in the towel so soon, Son. But also, be careful."

"Can I top you off?" he asked his father, taking the older man's cup and saucer while Amanda nodded her head. He made his way back to the kitchen and returned shortly thereafter.

"Dad, I've been meaning to ask you, what were the circumstances of Uncle Mike's death?"

Mr. Halloran was not expecting that question and gave himself some time to answer by taking a sip of coffee before placing the cup and saucer on the table between them.

"Mickey was killed while on duty. Shot. And as we've told you, nobody knows who did it. It was a different time and dishonest policemen were the rule, not the exception. We've always believed that he was trying to play by the rules he was taught, and someone didn't like that."

"Mickey? Is that what you called him?" Brendan asked.

"He changed it to Mike once he joined the force. He didn't want to be labeled a 'Mick.'"

"Fair enough," Brendan said, acknowledging the common appellation for an Irishman. "What was going on when he was on the force? Any issues in particular?"

"It wasn't the common 'taking a free apple off the cart' sort of thing. There were accusations of kickbacks and anyone who didn't turn a blind eye was considered a stool pigeon. It could be that his stern upbringing and strong morals were what brought him down."

"The current Chief probably served with Uncle Mike, don't you think?"

Mr. Halloran let out a brief noise. "Ha! Why don't you ask him about the good old days?"

"Dad—"

"That's enough of that sad story. Lucky for him your uncle wasn't married yet with a family left destitute. Now I'm done talking about it." He got up from the sofa, gave his son and Amanda a hug and went to the front door. "Sunday dinner tomorrow, remember?"

"Absolutely," Brendan said.

After his father left, he turned to his wife. "That's the most he's ever said about Mike."

"And it wasn't very much. Now we know why your parents are concerned about your safety. As am I."

"Being a detective is probably the safest place to be, in that case. No easy chances to bilk money from anyone I come into contact with," Brendan said, taking his father's cup and saucer into the kitchen.

Amanda followed him. "Maybe it's not just an apple or five dollars, but the stakes in this case are a lot higher. There's every chance someone will ask you to back off."

"Nobody has so far. They may think their standing in the community or their heritage is enough."

"Then they're very naïve if not downright stupid."

"Exactly," he said, putting his arms around her from behind.

The telephone rang.

"Great timing," he muttered, going back to the living room to answer it.

"Dominic, what's up?"

"Herb and I did a search of Mrs. Whiting's house."

"What did you find?"

"Some interesting letters in the late Spencer's desk drawer that we managed to see after a bit of jiggling from a letter opener suggesting he was about to default on a loan. Actually, several loans. One for the very large house in which he was living."

"Interesting."

"And several more unopened letters that seem to have come from the same banks. It looks like he stashed them in the locked drawer so nobody else would see them."

"Such as his wife?" Brendan asked.

"Yep."

"I sense that's not all."

"And our clever Clyde Owens came across Mrs. Whiting's discarded costume from the party in a bin in the kitchen."

"I don't blame her for ditching anything that reminded her of that evening."

"It had a piece of black fringe torn off the back."

Brendan was silent for a moment. Then, "Very good. I think it's time to talk to Mrs. Whiting again. She's still at her brother's place. I'll meet you there in a bit."

"Brendan, surely you're not going to go out there on a Saturday afternoon?" Amanda asked.

"Would you I rather go out on a Sunday? This can't wait. I'll be back in an hour or so."

Chapter 21

Brendan sat in his car outside the couple's house until he saw Dominic's car approach.

"Where's Clyde?" he asked, poking his head into the driver's side window.

"I dropped him at the station. He's got some religious instruction thing today."

"Really? Is he planning on becoming a minister?"

"Not exactly. Since he married my cousin, he's decided to join the Pope's team."

"I, for one, had him pegged all wrong when he first started. I took him for a know-it-all from Chicago whose department was so sick of him that they sent him our way. Whatever he was, it wasn't stupid and he adjusted pretty quickly in more ways than one."

"I wouldn't be surprised if Maria showed him the ropes."

"Now we have the origin of the black fringe in Spencer's hand. Possibly. We need to check all the other costumes to be sure," Brendan said.

Dominic let out a sigh. "Thirty people! I'll bet many of them threw away their costumes."

"You never know when you might be asked to be Robin Hood again, after all," Brendan said.

"With black fringe? What kind of costume was that?"

"Pretty strange, I can tell you. I got to the point of thinking my Wizard getup wasn't so bad after all. Well, are you ready?"

"Onward," Dominic said.

They stood patiently at the front door and after ringing the bell a second time, Anne came to answer it.

"Maid's half day," she said by way of greeting without inviting them in. "What can I help you with?"

"We need to speak with Mrs. Whiting."

"My husband is not here," she replied.

"We don't need to talk to him. We need to speak with her."

Anne heaved an exhausted sigh. "Come on in," she said. "I'll get her," and she left them in the small room where they had been seated previously, not offering to take their hats or coats nor to provide refreshment. They made themselves comfortable, looking around again at the décor that was certainly modern but nothing like the dramatic Whiting residence.

It was a good ten minutes before Anne reappeared with Bitsy at her heels, putting her hand to the back of her hair as if she had just risen from a nap and was patting it back into place.

"Do you want me to stay?" Anne asked her.

"Only if you want," Bitsy replied.

"I'll be just down the hall if you need me," she said and left abruptly.

"When is all the questioning going to be over?" Bitsy asked.

It wasn't the first thing Brendan had expected her to ask. She ought to have quizzed him about what progress they had made rather than how the investigation affected her. But she was grieving and maybe had been abruptly awakened from a nap, so he cut her some slack.

"Did your husband share any of his business dealings with you?"

She managed a small laugh. "The man was a whirlwind. Deals coming and going. Some came through, some did not. He may have mentioned some but I'm sure it was the tip of the iceberg of all that was going on at the company. Real estate can be fast-moving and ever-changing."

"I meant about your personal business dealings."

"What do you mean?"

"About the mortgage on the house, for example."

She furrowed her brow. "I knew we had a mortgage, but Spencer took care of all that sort of thing."

"You don't know the amount of the loan or the amount of the monthly payments?"

"Certainly not," she said. "Spencer did all that. Banks aren't interested in having a wife's signature on a loan. I probably couldn't get one on my own if I wanted to."

Brendan nodded, knowing that was true.

"Did he mention any property other than the house you owned?"

"He spoke incessantly about deals. 'We've got our eye on…' And by that I don't know if he meant he and Howard Hammond or if he was speaking of what he referred to as his team of agents. He liked to brag about the activity and the possibilities but he didn't go into detail with me. I suppose he thought I wasn't interested. And he was right. It could be a quite boring conversation when he referred to parts of the city or new subdivisions that I didn't recognize."

"Had he expressed any anxiety over your financial situation?"

Bitsy pulled her head back in surprise or offense. "Of course not! We were doing quite well. A brand-new house, a new car for me, club memberships rolled in—we were doing more than quite well, even if I didn't know where the money was coming from. Keep in mind that he was a broker and he got a portion of every commission that his team of agents made."

Brendan nodded in acknowledgment. "It must have been a lucrative business with that arrangement. But was there anything else on his mind that may have troubled him?"

She managed a laugh. "Spencer didn't let anything bother him. He could strut about and huff and puff, but nothing really got to him."

"We found evidence that some of the loans he had taken out were in default."

"What do you mean?" she asked, as if not knowing what they were talking about.

"The mortgage on the house was several months in arrears."

"That's not possible," she said stoutly.

"Is that what you argued about the night of the party?"

"How impertinent! How could we argue about something I knew nothing about?"

Brendan braced himself for the big blow. "Did you argue about him playing around with other women?"

Her face flushed but she said nothing.

"Do you know the name of the young woman he had been seeing?" he asked.

She leaned forward and pointed a finger at Brendan. "It's a man's world. And in business, there are always young women, ambitious women, who think they will get ahead by flirting with the boss. I've seen it time and again. They flatter him, they're with him all day long, with their painted nails and red lipstick. While the wife waits at home and her only occupation is her women friends or some idle hobby to make the days go by more quickly."

"So, do you think there was a young woman who was flattering him?"

"Yes, I do. It was that Shirley person. Very bold and forward in my opinion. She went from secretary to assistant in no time, and I'm sure she was thinking she was going to be the next Mrs. Whiting. Over my dead body!"

"Or his?" Brendan asked.

She paused. "I wouldn't have killed my husband for having succumbed to the advances of such a person. If anything, I would have thrown *her* down the stairs!"

"But you did argue?"

"We had words. Yes. I asked him to clear the staff out of the kitchen when I went to hide and, instead of finding a hiding place, I slipped in through the hall door. When I confronted him, he grabbed me by the shoulders and shook me as if to knock some sense into me and I pulled away. He even ripped part of my costume. I'd had enough of the drama at that point and, hearing the guests in the dining room doing the countdown, realized people were expecting the sardines game to begin. So, I went up the back stairs to the second floor and found my hiding place."

"Why did he go down to the basement?"

"I have no idea. There was nothing down there as far as I knew. The late Mr. Williams had a house full of furniture, but luckily nothing in the cellar. It's a huge empty space."

"Yes, I saw it."

"Can you imagine if it were filled from floor to ceiling with whatever people stuff in their cellars?"

"What do you keep in your basement?" Brendan asked.

Bitsy was startled by the question. "Spencer had some wine there, I think. The liquor stock wasn't in my domain."

Brendan felt he was at the end of the questioning, if not his own patience. "If there is anything else you can think of, no matter how small or insignificant, please call me." He handed her his card and her mouth twisted up to the side.

"I'll have my mind on finalizing the funeral arrangements. I don't think there's anything else I can tell you." With that, she got up and left the room, with Brendan and Dominic quickly getting up out of politeness, not that she had noticed. They took their outer garments and let themselves out of the house.

"Are you going back to the station?" Brendan asked.

"No, you?"

"I've had enough of today, and tomorrow I'm taking the whole day off.

Those were his words as he climbed into his car, but his mind was racing with the stories and alibis that everyone had told him. One thing stood out: Bitsy said she had played in the house when she was younger and he hit the steering wheel with his hand out of frustration that he had forgotten to ask her about Bill Williams. Did she realize he was at the party, or was the moustache and beard enough to disguise who he was? More importantly, she knew the house well not just from childhood but in planning the party while on site. She knew of the front stairs and back stairs and probably every secret hiding place. Could she have pushed Spencer down into the basement before she went to hide upstairs? He remembered his earlier remark of how ridiculous it was to imagine that small woman concocting the trip wire on the stairs. And now it didn't seem so absurd.

Chapter 22

The next day went by deliciously slowly with sleeping in, reading the thick Sunday **Boston Globe** and finally a filling mid-day dinner at Brendan's parents with no talk of work. It was a refreshing change from the hectic week and the constant turning over of clues and conversations from the week. All they talked about was the goings-on of family members and neighbors.

"Well?" Amanda asked as they drove home in the late afternoon.

"Well, what?"

"You have been entirely silent about the Whiting case all day."

"As intended," he said.

"Can you tell me what you found out from your chat with Bitsy yesterday?"

"I found out that she has had enough of my questions—although I forgot to ask her about the Williams family in more detail. Bill Williams said he and his date were a late addition to the guest list, so perhaps she didn't put two and two together. And I got the feeling she has had enough of the drama of her late husband, if I'm not being callous in putting it that way."

"There is a type of young woman who knows that the key to success in life is marrying well and then once that hurdle is achieved, they sit on their laurels."

"I love that mixed metaphor. Do you jump over a hurdle just to sit on some tree branches?" Brendan asked.

"Stop it," Amanda said, giving him a small swat on the arm. "For some women it seems that life almost ends at marriage. Mission accomplished. Now what to do? In Bitsy's case, it was taking art classes and throwing the occasional party for the sake of Spencer's ambitions."

"If you're correct, then that would be an argument absolving her of killing her husband."

Amanda turned to stare at him. "Do you seriously think she could have?"

"One point of view would suggest that, since she had reached her goal, she didn't have to do anything else. Except have children, perhaps. She could remain as idle as she wished. On the other hand, once achieving her goal, why did she need him anymore?"

"That's a very cold view of things," Amanda said.

"I agree. It's not my view, of course, and not yours, but it might have been hers. Spencer is gone, she inherits, and life resumes as a merry widow."

"Except it seems that she may not inherit all that much, from what you've said."

"True. But I don't think she knows that yet. I suspect Hammond was pushing the debt-riddled properties over to Spencer's side of the books and skimming the profits from the rest. It isn't clear to me what sort of partnership reporting went on."

"You're saying that Bitsy may have assumed she would be independently wealthy and not have to deal with a pesky husband?"

"Something like that." They had stopped at a red light and he looked over at her. "Do you know that she was taking art lessons? Or was it just something she told you?"

"She did show us a sketch," Amanda said. "And she has a room with art supplies where she seems to work."

"Could she have been carrying on with someone other than her husband?"

The light changed with a clang and he pulled forward.

"Brendan, this is the most disturbing conversation I've had with you."

"I'm not expressing my world view, merely observing how other people might see things and how they might act to achieve their goals."

They had finally arrived home and Amanda was still adjusting her reaction to her husband's observations.

"Do you feel like some tea?" he asked her, leaning over to kiss her on the cheek.

"That might be calming. Unless you're thinking of putting rat poison in it."

"Don't be silly. We don't have any rat poison."

"Put on the kettle and I'll get out of my Sunday dinner clothes into something more comfortable," she said, thinking of the cozy wool slacks that she hadn't worn since the previous weekend.

While Brendan was pottering in the kitchen, Amanda hung up her suit, and her eyes were caught by the dark mass at the bottom of the closet. She sighed impatiently. It was her costume from the Halloween party that had been discarded in haste and, being black, was somewhat invisible in the dark space. She pulled it out and wondered what in the world to do with it. Wear it next Halloween? Not likely. It was not in good shape, anyway. Part of the fringe was hanging off—how did that happen? Sloppy workmanship from Monsieur Josef's atelier? Or just too much work to be accomplished too quickly? If the fringe from her costume had come off so easily, perhaps that's what happened to Bitsy's fringe. Or someone else's. She turned the robe over to the back and saw how dirty it was. Of course, she had sat next to Bitsy in the hiding place during sardines. The Whitings might have had the house swept and dusted but someone forgot to pick up the drop cloth and clean underneath it.

She removed her stockings and garter belt and put on the lined wool slacks that were the essence of a weekend at home, looked for a pair of flat shoes and slipped them on. It wasn't until she had descended the stairs that an idea hit her.

"Bren, I've just thought of something that might be important."

"What is it?"

"I found my costume on the floor in the back of my closet and the fringe was partially torn. You said that was the case with Bitsy's outfit, too. Now I'm thinking that it didn't get torn in a scuffle with her husband. It might just have been that the costumes were hastily made or not made too well."

"I wouldn't let Louisa know your thoughts on that."

"And the back of my costume is covered in dust. Not from the floor of our closet, either. It's from the hiding place that Bitsy chose that someone forgot to clean before the guests arrived."

Brendan looked at her. "Okay, that all makes sense. But what of it?"

"There's something else nagging at me and I can't quite put my finger on it."

"Sit down, have some tea and let's listen to the radio. We've got a busy week ahead and I'll need to call everybody who was involved in the case in on Tuesday."

"All thirty people? And the staff, too?"

"No, it's going to be a much smaller group than that, I can assure you."

Chapter 23

Amanda was at the bank the moment it opened on Monday and asked to speak to Mr. Richardson. Disregarding Howard Hammond's wishes, she boldly requested the files for the Hammond & Whiting Property Management account rather than the firm's business account. The Vice-President looked at her quizzically, knowing that she was a private investigator but acquiesced as she had been there before and Hammond's name carried great weight.

"You're not the first one," he said raising one eyebrow.

He waved her into a small room and, after a short wait, several boxes were brought in. As she had expected, they were in reverse chronological order with the most recent transactions filed at the front. She thanked the young man who had delivered them and dug in.

Flipping through the sheets of paper, she saw initials at the top left that appeared to be those of whichever teller performed the transaction. But looking down to the bottom of each sheet, the signature was the same: Howard

Hammond. Reaching to the far end of the box, which dated back approximately six months, she began to make her list of the accounts from which funds were drawn and accounts into which money was transferred. At that point, she had no idea who owned what or if everything was shared investments between the two partners or if these properties were owned by outside investors. Nonetheless, she plowed on.

Five thousand dollars was withdrawn from the Brighton account and deposited to the Folsom account. She drew a line down the top sheet of the pad of paper she had brought with a minus sign on the left and a plus on the right side of the heading. B: $5,000 went on the left and F: $5,000 went on the right.

The transactions were made every few days and the amounts varied from a few hundred to several thousand. As she went through each transaction for one month, she saw that a reverse transaction hadn't taken place. In other words, F never put the $5,000 back into the B pot. Being cautious, she surmised that these might have been loans from one property or division or whatever it was to another, in which case she had to continue as far forward as she could to see if things balanced out. Someone had named the accounts from A to S, indicating there might have been nineteen accounts in existence although, as she continued, some of the letters of the alphabet were not represented. Did this mean they didn't exist or that there had been no activity?

It took Amanda well over two hours to compile the list of withdrawals and deposits and the sum at the bottom of her page three for deposits was staggering for that six-month period. Then she wondered where all that money had gone. Not back in individual property accounts but perhaps in the Hammond & Whiting business account. At this point, she did not have access to either Hammond's personal account or Whiting's and didn't think she'd be able to get it. Were they acting together to take funds from the profitable properties and melding them into an account of their own? Was Hammond cheating his partner, or was he cheating his investors? She had only scratched the surface of the complex web of transactions but it didn't look like an above-board business practice.

Amanda left and went to the station, hoping to catch Brendan at his desk. He sat with index cards with the guests' names on them scattered across the surface. Dominic was standing nearby and had picked up one card.

"I'm going with this one," he said.

"Oh, dear. I've found out something at the bank that might blow everything up," Amanda said.

Both men said in unison, "What?"

She sat down in the chair across the desk from Brendan. "I only went through six-months' worth of transactions for the Property Management division of the company and a lot of money was transferred out and not paid back in."

"What does that division oversee? Their own investments?"

"I'm not sure but probably not. There were close to twenty, which suggests that they were managing properties for investor groups or private individuals. I couldn't tell from what I saw."

"Maybe they were paying the profits out at the end of the week or the month," Dominic said.

"That's not usually how it works," Brendan said. "I can only speak from personal experience of my parents' small rental property. Not being millionaires, they watch the income and expenses like hawks each month, but they don't take that income and transfer it elsewhere."

"I can understand that," Dominic said. "But if you're managing multiple properties, you might need to get money from somewhere to cover unexpected costs."

"True, but you'd do that if they were all your properties. What if you're managing for someone else? Those accounts need to be kept separate."

"If that's what Hammond was doing, how long do you think he expected to get away with it until his actions were detected?" Amanda said.

"As long as Spencer and the investors didn't find out about it, he was safe. Now with his partner dead, he can blame any shady dealing on Whiting."

"Even if it he was the one doing it? Could he get away with saying he was instructed to do it by his partner?"

Amanda looked down at the index cards and, turning Hammond's over, saw that the words 'control' and 'competition' were written there. "And now we have another motive to add to the list: 'fear of discovery.'"

"I would love to see Howard Hammond's personal bank account. But if he's as smart as he is wily, then he'll have transferred the money from the property management accounts to a different bank. And he'll do his best to block us from seeing those records. What else have you got?" Amanda asked, picking up a separate stack of cards.

"Those are the people who we believe don't have any motive. Naturally, we are in that pile along with—well, see for yourself."

Shuffling through them she said, "The musicians?"

"They were in full sight of the guests the entire time. The pianist, for one, had his back to the kitchen and couldn't have seen anything of use to us. The bass player didn't leave his post until the evening was over and he had a clear sight line into the dining room. I think they're in the clear. Dominic interviewed them."

"They were hired by Mrs. Whiting on the recommendation of one of her friends. Otherwise, they didn't know the family at all. They said they didn't see anything unusual or suspicious during their time until the first scream."

"The assistants are in the clear?" Amanda asked.

"Why, what do you know that we don't?"

"You saw how Spencer yelled at one of them, calling him a name, when we were there for the closing on our new property."

"Plenty of people get called things at work. It doesn't turn them into murderers," Brendan said.

"What if Randy had some other reason to kill Spencer?"

"Such as?"

"Shirley let slip that it made sense that Randy served as bartender that night because Spencer told her he used to do that job."

"So what?" Dominic said.

"In a men's club."

"Yeah, so?"

"A men's club that catered to other men, if you get my meaning. Older men. Younger men," Amanda said.

Brendan and Dominic exchanged glances.

"Do you think that was enough motivation for Randy to toss his employer down the stairs?" Dominic asked.

"Shouldn't he have thrown Shirley down the stairs for spreading gossip?" Brendan asked.

"How likely would he want to kill his employer?" Amanda asked.

Brendan took the card from her and laid it on the table with the group of possible suspects. They continued to look them over while she shuffled through the group considered unlikely.

"What about Bill Williams?" she asked.

"Aside from the fact that he disguised himself and somehow got invited to the party, what reason would he have for killing Spencer? The fact his father disowned him, as far as I know, had nothing to do with Spencer," Brendan said.

"All right. But here's a thought. What if Spencer wasn't the intended victim? What if someone else was supposed to go down the basement step?"

"Such as?"

"Howard Hammond. What if Bitsy figured out the skimming situation and told her husband. Spencer was supposed to lure him to the basement. Wasn't Bitsy actually shocked that her husband had died?"

"You mean the two men wrestled with one another in the kitchen after the staff has been cleared out and the wrong man fell to his death?" Brendan asked.

"It's possible, isn't it?" Amanda asked.

"It seems anything is possible. A few issues with that scenario: Bitsy claimed up and down that the Whiting family was solvent—even prosperous. She made it seem like she didn't involve herself in financial affairs. How would she know more about the finances than her husband? And then, she admitted that she confronted Spencer about his philandering when they were alone in the kitchen. That could have led her to lash out with deadly results. Dominic, I think it's time to get all these folks in here first thing tomorrow morning. We've got too many questions and not enough answers."

After Dominic left, Amanda said, "There's somebody we're not looking at, I'm sure. Do you remember me telling you about my dirty costume from sitting in the dust at the Williams house? I would have expected everyone to have had that same imprint on the back of their costumes. I certainly noticed it with Bitsy's when she came downstairs, as well as the Wolf, Red Riding Hood and Louisa's outfit. But I just remembered that somebody there had an utterly clean costume. There's the crux of the matter. I'll tell you when we get home."

Over a dinner of tomato soup and grilled cheese sandwiches, one of Amanda's latest specialties, she outlined her thought process. They went back and forth poking holes with questions at the suppositions made and the evidence to support it.

"Well, it's possible, isn't it?" Amanda asked as they both cleared the table.

"Wash or dry?" he asked. She filled up the sink with hot water and a scoop of the grated Fels-Naptha that she stored in a jar under the sink.

"I'll wash," she said.

With just the two of them and a simple meal, the chore was done quickly and the dishes dried and put away.

"I'm going to take a bath and go to bed early," Amanda said, giving Brendan a kiss on the cheek.

"I'm going to listen to the fight." Brendan glanced at his watch. "It's on in ten minutes." He went into the living room and turned on the radio.

"Just not too loud," Amanda said, knowing that even if he kept the volume down, he was an enthusiastic and vocal fan.

HOURS LATER, Amanda woke up and padded in bare feet to the bathroom. She flipped the switch but the light didn't come on. She wasn't about to go searching for a replacement bulb in the middle of the night, so did her best to find her way around in the dark. Walking back to the bedroom, she smashed her toe against the wall and yelped. She could see Brendan pop up in the dim bedroom and instantly regretted having called out.

He leaned over to the nightstand on his side of the bed to click on the light.

"What happened?" he asked her before saying, "What the heck—has the electricity gone out?"

"I went to the bathroom and I thought the bulb had burned out. And smacked my toe. Let me try my light," she said, able to see the outline of the night table. She tried clicking the switch on and off.

"That's annoying," Brendan said, pulling the covers off. "I don't suppose we have a flashlight up here?"

"There's one in the kitchen."

He heaved a sigh and got into his slippers and felt his way out of the room onto the landing. As he proceeded down the stairs, he caught sight of something bright outside the front door. A fire was merrily burning right outside the front door, fueled by the adjacent leaf litter and pine needles.

"There's a fire!" he yelled. "Call the fire department! Or ask the operator to call them."

Amanda picked up the upstairs extension and heard no dial tone. She looked at the receiver and pounded down on instrument's buttons as if that would bring it back to life.

Brendan had raced down the stairs, fumbled with the lock and flung the door open, only to crash into the wooden bench that had been moved to block his way. Having scraped his shins, he climbed over and stamped out the fire as best he could.

Amanda came running down the stairs in her bare feet. "Brendan, the phone is dead."

She stopped short inside the front door and watched as he spread the remaining embers of the fire out.

"I'll get some water," he said, pushing the bench out of the way. She stood looking at the mess on the ground until he came back with a pitcher of water and splashed it on what remained. The sizzling told them the fire was out and they looked at one another.

"None of this was an accident. The power going out, the phone line probably cut and this stupid bench put in the way so I would go head over heels into the flames. At least it looks like it had just got going. We're lucky it didn't spread to the wooden sidings," he said, looking back at their house. "Come on, let's try to get some sleep. It's cold and there you're in your bare feet."

Amanda looked down and suddenly the image of bare feet clicked in her brain. "Brendan, I think we're on the right track."

Chapter 24

Brendan had considered assembling everyone back at the Williams house for the striking effect it would have on the guilty party but realized that some folks might be so disturbed by the setting that it could provoke emotions that would provide cover for the real culprit. Instead, he had the large conference room at the station made available with enough seats to accommodate the group contained in his index card pile. The conversation with Amanda the night before was enlightening and opened the door to so many other motives and opportunities. And what a clever culprit it had been—if they were correct.

Bitsy came in, solemnly dressed in black, accompanied by her brother, Bruce, and his wife, Anne, who had a peeved expression as if to say she had no idea why she was called to this meeting in addition to being fed up with housing her sister-in-law. Howard Hammond came in separately from Shirley, although he had given her a ride there, as if to send a message that they may have been a couple on the night of the party but they were not an item. From the expressions on their faces, that was the message that Hammond wanted to send, but Shirley smiled and sat next to him as if that wasn't the case. Bill Williams had been called in along with his date for that evening, as were Julia and George, formerly referred to as Red Riding Hood and the Wolf.

Brendan needed to provide some padding for the assembled group so had also asked Louisa, Rob, Caroline and José to come in. José had been in the bar with Brendan and Rob but Louisa and Caroline had been upstairs engaged in the sardines game. The Sun and Moon couple came in late, looking as if they had no idea why they had been called to the assembly. Spencer's two male assistants and the women who worked in the kitchen crept in, wide-eyed and hesitant to think they might be under suspicion.

Brendan began to speak. "Thank you for being here. I know this is a dreadful business and I'm sure Spencer Whiting's family would like us to come to a conclusion about what exactly happened the night of the party. I believe you know who I am, since I interviewed many of you and I was also present at the party. My wife, Amanda, is a private investigator and has been of invaluable help in this." He gestured to the side of the room where she sat. "Dominic Barone has assisted me in an official capacity and we've asked you here to review what we know to date."

Bitsy took out a handkerchief and dabbed at her eyes.

"From what I have been led to believe, Spencer Whiting and Howard Hammond, old friends, had a prosperous partnership based on jovial and healthy competition. The Whitings had a strong, stable relationship. They had a wide circle of friends who were as prosperous as they were and he felt he was on the brink of selling the Williams mansion. This was the surface view of things. But it wasn't reality."

Several people looked confused by his statement, but he continued.

"Before I talk about that, let's go back to the sequence of events. The party was in full swing, music was playing, dancing was lively, guests were eating and drinking. And then Bitsy, Mrs. Whiting, had a series of parlor games—bobbing for apples, charades and the mummy wrapping event." There were a few meager smiles as they reminisced.

"Then Mrs. Whiting announced the game of sardines and asked the guests to count slowly to one hundred while she found her hiding place. And she mentioned that everyone should turn around so they couldn't see which direction she took. That was an important stage direction from her."

Bitsy looked puzzled at his last comment.

"Not everyone went looking for Mrs. Whiting. There was a contingent who stayed in the dining room drinking, eating and listening to the music. It was quite some time before we heard a shriek from the kitchen and everyone downstairs piled into that room. The others who had been searching upstairs also came down, as did Mrs. Whiting and the people who had found her.

Those were the Wolf and Little Red Riding Hood, Cleopatra, the Queen and the Witch. Is that correct?"

Those who he had named nodded in agreement.

"It seemed that Spencer Whiting shooed the staff out of the kitchen earlier and, for reasons we don't understand, went to the basement, tripped on the wire strung across the third step and fell to his death."

Bitsy employed her handkerchief, again dabbing at her eyes.

"That was what seemed to occur. But we've made a lot of suppositions. Everyone assumed that Mrs. Whiting went upstairs to hide, although she asked people not to peek. What if she instead went around to the other entrance to the kitchen from the hallway to confront her husband about something?"

Bitsy looked down at her lap.

"Who else could have got to the kitchen without anyone else noticing? Mr. Hammond said he wasn't feeling well and was in the bathroom at the end of the hall. The hall that had a door to the kitchen. He wasn't in the dining room with us or looking for Mrs. Whiting by his own admission. But was he in the bathroom?"

Howard Hammond crossed his hands over his chest and scowled.

"The two assistants, Randy and Reggie, were busy behind the bar and at the table, but did anyone notice if they slipped into the kitchen to get ice? And possibly out the other door to the hall?"

They remained stone-faced at the implication.

"And there was an interesting guest at the party, the son of the former owner."

Everyone looked around the room until Bitsy finally recognized her old playmate. "Bill! I would never have recognized you."

He managed a small smile.

"With so many people and moving pieces, I have no recollection of where the Devil was all evening, only noticing his diabolical beard and moustache when everyone's mask came off. I also didn't track where the Cop and Robber were during the event."

Bruce stood up to leave. "This is pointless." His wife pulled him back down to a seated position.

"We talked about Caesar, but where was Cleopatra during all this? She was among the first to find Bitsy and sat there under the drop cloth until the screaming began."

Brendan paused.

"That is what seems to have happened and where people seemed to be. More importantly, what possible motives were at work for someone to have devised that trip wire? We've recently found out that the Hammond & Whiting business was doing well, with one partner doing very much better than the other. It wasn't due to the skill of the sales pitch or expertise in choosing the right investment vehicle. It seems Mr. Hammond was busy at various banks in town moving money from their jointly owned property management venture. As was explained to me, Spencer was the rainmaker, the person who brought in the clients, and Howard was the numbers man. In looking at those transactions in the property management division, only Hammond's initials are on the withdrawal slips. The money got transferred from one account to another and likely ended up only in one person's pockets."

"What are you suggesting?" Hammond said, his face stern.

"I am saying that you were cheating your partner."

"I'll have my lawyer sue you for defamation."

"It isn't defamation if it's the truth. And somehow Spencer found out about it before the night of the party and you had angry words about it. There was at least one witness to it. You could have very easily slipped away from your alleged long visit to the bathroom and gone into the kitchen, only to see Spencer there alone. A perfect opportunity."

"If he only found out about it the night of the party, I wouldn't have had the opportunity to set the trip wire, would I?' he asked triumphantly.

"No. Somebody else did."

That startled everyone in the room.

"Barton, the Sun, had dealings with Spencer in the past and didn't come out of it very well, as he told me. He could have been the one to booby trap the stairs."

"That's ridiculous," Barton said. "I had the most conspicuous outfit of anyone there. I saw you, and presumably you saw me, sitting in the corner with that stupid headpiece on, nursing a drink."

"But where was Deborah, your wife? Upstairs looking for Bitsy? Or luring Spencer to the door to the basement?"

"I'd never met the man before in my life!" she said.

"No, but Barton could have pointed him out to you although he didn't have to. It was clear from the beginning of the party who the host and hostess were. Barton certainly knew where the party was to be held, and he could have set up the trap earlier in the day before you both got there."

She looked at her husband, evidently recalling the moment he realized who their hosts were.

"The happy faces that the Whiting couple put on masked a troubled marriage. The big issue was Spencer's philandering habit. One of his trysts was with Shirley Butler, his assistant, which she told my wife and me about after the party."

Shirley had the grace to look embarrassed.

"It seems that Mrs. Whiting already knew—probably told to her by the young woman herself, if only to gloat—and Bitsy confronted Spencer when she was supposed to be hiding. That would seem to be enough motive to do away with her spouse. If she had been aware of their dire financial situation with a huge mortgage on their house and his partner skimming the proceeds, she would have been a great deal angrier."

"It occurred to me that her brother Bruce might have caught wind of the difficulties and come to the rescue of his sister. But after talking with him, he has his feet planted firmly in his own interests and would not have gone to such lengths to seek revenge for her."

"So, we have many people with motives to want to do away with Spencer Whiting. But there is one person who stood to lose the most," He paused. "Our young friend, Shirley Butler."

"What?" she said, truly startled.

"She thought she could secure her job by having an affair with the boss. But once he realized his wife suspected or knew about it, he broke off the relationship. Shirley could live with that, but she couldn't live with the ultimatum that she leave the employ of Hammond & Whiting.

She had worked long and hard to get where she was and she decided she was going nowhere. What better resolution than to do away with the boss? Nobody else knew that she was going to have to leave her job. And that left Howard Hammond as fair game for her next conquest."

"That's stupid. I was in full view of everyone, especially his wife!" Shirley said.

"That's where you were very clever. Your costume as Cleopatra was very simple—a rectangle of cloth pinned at the shoulders and cinched with a belt. Monsieur Josef's staff put it together and it was easily replicated. You told your long-time friend, Gretchen, that you wanted to play a little joke on her boss and you told her all about the layout of the Williams house and her small part in the prank."

Brendan nodded to Dominic, who left the room and came back with Gretchen, who was puzzled by her own presence.

Shirley turned and glared at her. "What are you doing here?" she said in a loud whisper.

"I'm not sure."

"What was the prank that Shirley asked you to take part in?" Brendan asked.

Gretchen began hesitantly, intimidated by the gathering. "She knew that one of the games was for people to be able to identify who was behind each mask at the end of the evening. She said it would be funny that, when it came to be the turn for Cleopatra to remove her mask, Mr.

Hammond would be astonished to find out it wasn't Shirley but that it was me."

"That's not very funny," Hammond said.

"But the afternoon of the party, she said she changed her mind and that if I heard a scream while I was hiding with Mrs. Whiting, I should get out of the sardines hiding place, put on my coat and get out of the house as soon as possible. She didn't say why, just that it was a prank," Gretchen said.

Brendan took up the narrative. "It wasn't meant to be. Both young women are the same height and build with the same shoulder-length dark hair. They could easily be mistaken for one another. That's what Shirley was counting on. She told Gretchen about the sardines game and had her in the duplicate Cleopatra costume, waiting upstairs for Bitsy to come up and secure a hiding spot. Just as Shirley had predicted, the hostess dove under the drop cloth. And once the group downstairs yelled out that they had reached one hundred, Gretchen slowly came out of her hiding spot and went directly to where Mrs. Whiting was hidden. They both couldn't talk or it would give away the hiding place, but Mrs. Whiting was shooting daggers with her eyes at Gretchen thinking it was Shirley."

"Oh, I wondered why she looked so cross," Gretchen said.

"Other guests found them and they waited for more until they heard the scream from downstairs and they all ran out. Gretchen stayed behind, put on her overcoat and came down the stairs and out the front door."

"That's ridiculous. She would have been seen," Shirley said.

"No, everyone had already filled up the kitchen, their attention drawn by the shriek. Reggie had abandoned his post at the front door long before to help Randy at the bar. Even the musicians had left their instruments to crowd around. She left completely undetected."

"So, who killed Spencer?" Bitsy asked, perplexed by the appearance of the unknown girl and her role in the tragedy.

"Why, Shirley of course. When the masks came off, there was Shirley dressed as Cleopatra, who even Spencer's widow could testify had been upstairs hiding with her."

"It *was* me hiding with her," Shirley insisted. "You can't prove it wasn't."

"Three things can prove it wasn't. First, the crumpled-up, discarded duplicate costume in the bottom of Gretchen's closet. With a big patch of dust at the back indicating where she had sat. Everyone who found Bitsy had dusty costumes from that location. But your costume was pristine. The other thing was, when Amanda and Louisa joined the hiding group, Cleopatra moved over and tucked her bare feet under her costume. Shirley had sandals on to complete her outfit and didn't have the forethought to get a pair for her old pal, Gretchen, who only brought street shoes with her. The last and most important fact is that Gretchen just exposed your lie."

"Here's how Shirley did it. While the sardines game was in full swing, she went into the kitchen to confront Spencer one last time about her job and their relationship. She had already assumed that he would not relent and had put the trip wire up earlier in the day when the final preparations for the party were being made. When she got no positive results from her arguments with him, she might have told him that he was correct in prohibiting guests from going into the basement. Curious, he might have asked why, only to open the door and get pushed down the stairs. She could have gone up the back stairs and hidden, only to reappear once the body was discovered."

"You can't prove any of this," Shirley said.

"I strongly suspect that as more people were questioned, you thought Gretchen might spill the beans." Looking at the others present he said, "Don't you think it was an unusual accident to have Shirley bring her sick friend home from work and later the gas heater was on full blast, emitting lethal carbon monoxide into the room?"

Gretchen gasped. "You couldn't have done that on purpose, could you?"

Shirley did not make eye contact.

"But why?" Gretchen persisted.

"Why what?"

"Why everything? We've known each other for years. And you're my annoying shadow. Copying everything I do, how I look, how I dress, even where I work. I was desperate to get out of our stupid little hometown and get rid of you. But I couldn't go by myself. My parents wouldn't let me. So, my shadow followed, reminding everyone of our small-town roots. Moping around about her life, whining instead of going out and getting something of her own." Looking at Bitsy, she said, "And that husband of yours was a total creep. He started the whole thing and it dawned on me, why not play into it. I'd get a better job and, if he got tired of me, so what? I could always hold it over his head."

"You wouldn't have been the first one, Dear," Bitsy said. "He'd repented in the past, then behave himself before starting up with someone new. He was a serial cheater and I don't know why, for the life of me, I put up with it so long."

Brendan looked at the young woman. "Shirley Butler, I'm arresting you for the murder of Spencer Whiting. I don't have the necessary proof to charge you with the attempted murder of your old friend. And if I feel benevolent, I might ignore your act of vandalism on our house last night, cutting off the electricity as well as the telephone. Oh, yes. There's also an arson charge."

Shirley gripped the seat of her chair, looking around for somebody, anybody, to help her before glancing back at the door to the hall as if she were going to make an attempt at an escape. The sheer number of people that sat between her and any means of escape deflated her and she slumped in her chair.

"It isn't fair," were her last words before Dominic took her by the arm and led her from the room.

Chapter 25

"You noticed nobody thanked me," Brendan said when Amanda and Dominic were back in his office later that day.

"How could they? Mrs. Whiting had her late husband's shabby infidelities highlighted, as well as his shocking financial situation," Amanda said.

"And then you also managed to expose Howard Hammond's scheme, whatever that was. I imagine some of his investors will come thundering down on him once word gets out that he was moving their money around without their knowledge," Dominic said.

"There really weren't any other viable suspects except for that Barton fellow, but he impressed me as more of a talker than an action person," Brendan said. "The assistants may have carried grudges, too, but they could hardly kill the goose that laid the golden egg—Spencer and their jobs. It seems they've landed on their feet and, with Shirley out of the picture, perhaps one of them will pick up her spot."

"I feel sorry for the son, Bill Williams," Dominic said. "Sounds like his father was a nasty piece of work."

"I was asking my father more about that situation," Amanda said. "He said that in this state, a parent has to clearly exclude an adult child by name in order for that person not to have any claim. If the older man just omitted naming him at all, suggesting that he had no offspring, Bill may have grounds to get something. Or if there was some undue influence in drafting the will or if the person was not of 'sound mind.' And my father also said that the elder Mr. Williams purposefully hired a young attorney with no knowledge of the family to assist in drafting his will. That might have been an attempt to evade the relationship."

"Well, perhaps there is hope for him, after all, in an appeal."

"I'm starting to question our taking on tenants now that I know what can go wrong," Amanda said.

"Too late, now, my dear," Brendan said.

"There are the interruptions during the workday and the unexpected repairs. The tensions among the tenants and our lack of privacy."

"Nobody expects a cold-blooded murderer. Certainly not one that's a small-town, young woman," Brendan said.

"How are the roommates taking it?" Dominic asked.

"Rebecca and Dassie were not involved with the other two. And none of them had been there that long. But still, it's chilling and I think we'll have to install locks on each of the bedroom doors for their peace of mind."

"We'll get on it this weekend," Brendan said. "I bet my father would love to help out."

"What about Gretchen? That had to have been a terrific blow," Dominic asked.

"I believe she'll rebound well. You'll never believe it, but she pulled me aside as everyone was leaving and asked if she could have Shirley's old room!"

∼

Next: A CHRISTMAS MURDER MYSTERY
The annual society holiday charity ball held at a grand mansion ends abruptly
with a murder and a locked room mystery.

To keep up with new releases please visit my website and sign up for my newsletter.
www.Andreas-books.com

©**ANDREA KRESS 2025**

Printed in Dunstable, United Kingdom